LAST
CHANCE
SUMMER

LAST CHANCE SUMMER

Shannon Klare

Swoon
READS

Swoon Reads New York

A SWOON READS BOOK
An Imprint of Feiwel and Friends and Macmillan Publishing Group LLC
120 Broadway, New York, NY 10271

Our books may be purchased in bulk for promotional, educational,
or business use. Please contact your local bookseller or the Macmillan
Corporate and Premium Sales Department at (800) 221-7945 ext. 5442
or by email at MacmillanSpecialMarkets@macmillan.com.

Library of Congress Control Number: 2019948839
ISBN 978-1-250-31364-5 (hardcover) / ISBN 978-1-250-31365-2 (ebook)

Book design by Trisha Previte

First Edition—2020

10 9 8 7 6 5 4 3 2 1

swoonreads.com

For Macy and Blake
Never be afraid to follow your dreams.

LAST
CHANCE
SUMMER

Prologue

March

"You're coming, right? You have to come. Why am I even asking this question? You're totally coming."

"You know I can't," I said, repeating myself for the third time.

Ahead, taillights on a double-parked Prius flashed to life. Nikki slowed beside the driver's side, her brown eyes assessing me behind oversized sunglasses.

"You could," she said, ignoring me for the millionth time. "You're just too scared."

My hand wrapped around the blistering passenger-side handle, my feet unmoving. "My parents would have a full-on meltdown," I said, opening the door. "I can't. Final answer."

I slid into the passenger seat, suffocated by thick Louisiana heat. The minute Nikki turned the key in the ignition, I reached for the temperature knob. The lowest setting blew hot through the vents, shifting colder as she reversed from the spot.

"Everyone will be there," she said after a pause, joining a row of cars exiting the mall. "Don't be the girl who doesn't go."

"I'm still grounded," I said, scowling. "Today was an exception."

She tapped her fingers against the steering wheel, her face tilting my way. "Then sneak out."

Not on my worst day was sneaking out an option. She would know that, had she paid attention the last three months.

I shook my head.

"Why are you trying to ruin my night?" she groaned.

"Why are *you* being such an inconsiderate friend?" I shifted toward her, the leather seat burning the back of my legs. "It's easy for you to sit over there and judge me, but you've never experienced this level of grounding. Stop for point-five seconds and put yourself in my shoes."

"I'm trying," she said, turning onto a side road. "But I'm having major friendship withdrawals. Do you realize my only wingwoman is Brooke? She doesn't even use makeup primer. Beauty sin numero uno."

"She isn't that bad."

"She isn't you," Nikki said. She turned the air conditioner from low to mid-seventies, frowning, stewing quietly in the driver's seat. "How much longer do you have, anyway? Is it until the end of the month, or end of the school year?"

"End of the month," I said.

The two-story mall disappeared behind us, our all-day shopping trip my first nonschool outside interaction in weeks.

Confined to the Reynolds's fortress of solitude, my long-term house arrest left me clinging to legitimate social interaction like it was essential to survive. The sooner the grounding ended, the quicker I could go back to my normal life with a less-complainy version of Nikki.

"That will take forever," she said after a minute. "I can't suffer that long."

"You aren't the one suffering. I'm the one getting an endless string of texts from half the junior class. Everyone wants to know where I'm at and why I'm not coming. Like they don't know," I said.

"Then skip your all-night painting sesh and get back into the scene," Nikki said. "You haven't been around since Thanksgiving, Alex. I know you're trying to follow the rules or whatever, but this grounding is going to ruin your rep."

"Again, it isn't my choice," I said, grabbing a nude lip-gloss from my bag.

Nikki's laser focus and unbending willpower may have gotten her what she wanted 90 percent of the time, but no one could match my stubbornness.

"It could be," she said.

"But it's not."

Her lips spread into a thin line as her manicured nails reached for the radio. "Fine. Be a party pooper."

"Fine. I will."

I swiped the gloss across my lips and tossed it back into the bag, glancing at my phone as it lit up inside.

Mitch: Where are you?

"I can't handle you too," I groaned.

Mitch Watson could go to hell in a handbasket. The sooner, the better.

"Handle who?" Nikki said, swerving far enough to the left to earn a blast of a horn.

I nudged her, my eyes darting to the road. "Could you stay in your lane for literally five seconds?" I said.

"Metaphorically or literally?" she said, grinning. She motioned to the phone, shades of mischief crossing her freckled face. "Based on your attitude, it has to be Mitch. Is he still blowing up your phone?"

"Has been since yesterday," I said. "You'd think he'd eventually get the point. As far as I'm concerned, he can go back to LSU and leave me alone."

"That's my girl!" Nikki said, nudging me from across the console. "Boy didn't know what he had. You're better off without him."

"Truth," I said, more to myself than Nikki. "Any boy who takes more than three months to realize he messed up doesn't deserve me. It's time to move on to someone better. Smarter."

"Better-looking and preferably the captain of a sports team," she added.

My phone lit again; another text from my only ghost of boyfriends past. Mitch was my own personal Jeff Probst, eagerly waiting to snuff out my torch. One inch and he'd kill the light. Not today, Satan. Not today.

"So, back to the actual topic," she said. "I'm starting a petition for your freedom. You need your life back and I need you. Your parents can either jump on the fun train or get run over by it."

"I wish it was that easy."

Nikki continued along the interstate, entering and exiting parishes until Crighton's massive metal sign welcomed us home. The town, consisting of no more than 2,500 people, died with the loss of steam engines. Its former glory boiled down to one severely dwindled ghost town and one mediocre McDonald's.

She pulled off the interstate and onto Crighton's cobblestoned main street. Cracked brick buildings held 75 percent of the town's businesses. My mom's salon sat at end of the street, her Equinox gleaming pewter beneath the sun.

"What if you told them you were sleeping over at my house?" Nikki said, eyeing the SUV. "We could sneak out after my grandma goes to bed, drive to the party, and no one has to know. As long as we're in before the sun comes up, it will be like it never happened."

"I'm not scamming your grandma," I said, sighing. "She's literally the nicest old lady in town. I would feel morally wrong."

"It's not like she would know. She goes to bed at a quarter after six and rarely wakes up before sunrise. We'll be back before she knows we're gone."

"I've messed up more than enough to know no plan is foolproof," I said, shaking my head.

"Okay, but at the risk of sounding judgmental, where was *that* moral guide when Mitch was the one asking you to go have some fun?"

I paused, my jaw slightly ajar. "That's not fair," I said.

"I'm sorry," Nikki said. "I'm not trying to be harsh. I'm just trying to save you from senior year hell. You do remember what it was like to be socially isolated, right? We were miserable. I can't do that again."

I gnawed on my lip, the truth a cruel reminder of what was at stake. Of course I remembered. Being the sheriff's daughter branded me with a stigma from the start. I was too wholesome. Too dangerous to include. No one wanted to risk getting caught at a party. No one wanted to risk me ratting them out.

Until Mitch.

A few minutes later, Nikki stopped at the curb outside my house. The brick-and-limestone exterior contrasted dark wood accents, dark shutters, and espresso-colored porch rails. The manicured lawns, freshly mowed by my dad, left it a picture of perfection. From the outside, my family seemed like a put-together piece of art. In reality, our relationships were as raw as the exposed drywall and paint swatches left from remodeling.

I unbuckled my seat belt and retrieved my shopping bags. "Can I call you later?" I said, opening the door.

"Yeah," she said. "Just make sure you start the call with *I'm spending the night at your house.*"

"You really should take up debate," I said, stepping onto the curb. "You could channel your persuasive powers for good, not evil."

"Why would I do that?" she said. "Villains have all the fun."

I grinned and closed the door, hauling shopping bags across the concrete path. The wooden porch creaked the minute I stepped onto it; the large front door squealed on its hinges. Inside the foyer, paint fumes hung thick in the air. I held my breath, heading for the stairs.

My room was first on the right, a collection of everything a "popular kid" should have. A lighted vanity with too much makeup? Check. One massive closet with too many clothes? Check. Mounted TV with speaker system? Check.

The room was full of things I'd asked for, but none of it made a difference in gaining me credit. One night of rebellion did more for my reputation than anything expensive ever could.

I dropped the shopping bags inside my door, glancing at an easel near the window. The sunset backdrop I'd worked on for two days was almost complete. Painting was the best distraction from my grounding, but you could only paint the same scene once or twice before it got old.

I turned, sighing as I pulled my phone from my purse and synced it with a Bluetooth speaker across the room. Texts from Mitch continued to flash across the screen, each apology a new knife to the gut.

I took a seat on my bed, staring at little white lights scattered in a canopy above me. For all his faults, Mitch loved me when no one else could see me as anything but the sheriff's daughter. He was my confidant in too many situations. My best friend. And, despite the blow he dealt to my heart, I couldn't pretend I didn't care. I always would.

My heart cinched in my chest. Oxygen burned my lungs, while tears stung my eyes. I hadn't cried in months. He wasn't worth crying over anymore.

"Damn it," I said, blinking them back.

I heaved in a long breath and dragged myself off the bed, shaking my head as I crossed the room. In the vanity mirror, a put-together mess watched me cross the room. Her blue eyes, barely blemished porcelain skin, and curled blond hair were an image. They weren't reality. No one really knew me. Except Nikki.

I stopped in front of the vanity, placing my palms flush against the wood. Lying to her grandma was wrong on so many levels, but I hadn't been at a party in months. The longer I stayed out of the scene, the more irrelevant I became. Despite arguing with her, Nikki's words were fact. Going to this party was more of a *had to* than anything. I had to go. End of story.

I headed for my bed, grabbing the phone from the comforter. My mom's text stream was third on the list. I hit her name with my thumb, typing at rapid speed.

> **Me:** Will you ask dad if I can spend the night at Nikki's?

I hit send, my heart beating out of my chest as three little dots blinked across the screen.

> **Mom:** You're still grounded.

"Mom," I groaned, typing a response. She was smart not to trust me. Half the time I couldn't trust myself.

I sat on the chair at my vanity, forearms resting against my knees.

> **Me:** And I haven't asked to stay over at Nikki's since November.
> **Mom:** Your dad is the one you need to ask. Not me.
> **Me:** We both know dad will say no. Please mom. :(

"This was a stupid idea," I said, shaking my head. Getting her to agree to a day out with Nikki was a gift. No way she'd agree to this too.

Mom: I love you, but no.

And there it was: rejection.

I sat the phone on the vanity, scowling at my reflection. I had sacrificed too much to get to this point. Letting my popularity slip away would be stupid. With or without permission, I was going to that party.

* * *

A quarter past nine, I snuck through my window on the top floor. My shoes slid across roof tiles, the moonless night giving me little light to work with.

Two blocks away, Nikki's car sat beneath the glow of a streetlamp. I landed on the grass a few minutes later, clutching a pair of sandals as I sprinted toward her car.

My hand rapped against the car's window, loud in the quiet of the night. She immediately hit the unlock button, stowing her phone beneath the radio as I slid inside.

"Two things," she said, holding up a pair of fingers. "First, I love your shirt. Second, you're late."

"I know. I know," I breathed, clicking my seat belt. "But you try sneaking out when your parents check on you every ten minutes. I swear it's like I'm living in the *Big Brother* house."

"Where's Julie Chen when you need her?" Nikki said, putting the car in drive.

"So, how did you manage to get out?" she asked, pulling a Styrofoam cup from the cup holder. "Back door? Window?"

"I snuck out the window and almost broke myself in the process," I said, slipping into my sandals. "I swear that rainstorm was sent to kill me."

"Well, roofs are wet when it rains," Nikki said after a minute. "Maybe you should've tried the door."

"Next time I'll remember that," I said.

I glanced at the thick row of trees outside my neighborhood. The lakeside views were gorgeous, but hidden behind too many cypress trees. At night, mosquitoes swarmed the shorelines. Baker's Swamp would be worse.

"Oh! I did remember bug spray," I said, digging in my purse for the bottle of Off!

"Bug spray is good, but I have something better," Nikki said, handing me the cup. "Five sips of that and you won't even notice the bugs."

I took a sip. Vodka burned its way down my throat, making me gag. "Geez, Nikki. Would you like some fruit juice with your vodka?" I said, handing it back.

"You think I put too much in?" she said, returning the cup to the holder. "I thought it was good! Had two before I left the house, actually. And I'm happy to report that so far there are no serious side effects. Except for a buzz, I'm feeling pretty good over here."

I rolled my eyes. Nikki was never one to pass on a drink, but she usually gave me warning before we went somewhere.

"If I knew you were drinking, I would've kicked you out of the driver's seat," I said, shifting toward her. "I'm totally fine being the designated driver."

"I'm fine to drive!" she said, waving me off. "You know I can down at least four vodka sours before I start feeling them. Hashtag, tolerance."

"Hashtag, irresponsible," I said, shaking my head.

"Besides, it isn't that strong," she said. "It's vodka fruit punch or something. The juice waters it down. No worries."

"Famous last words," I muttered, staring out the window again.

Trees outside grew thicker with each passing mile. When Nikki turned down a country road ten miles later, I pulled a tube of lip-gloss from my bag. She pulled off the road shortly after, the flicker of firelight amplifying as we drove through a line of trees.

Baker's Swamp was bursting with cars and occupied by what seemed to be 90 percent of Crighton High's student body. With a town as slow as ours, it wasn't surprising to see this many people at the party. Still, my nerves stood on end. Anxiety and anticipation mixed with excitement.

Nikki wedged her Prius behind a Mustang, leaving barely three inches between my door and an all-too-familiar Chevy. I eyed the truck as I slid through the opening, my pulse quickening at the LSU parking tag in the window—Mitch.

"Come on, slowpoke," Nikki said, slipping through vehicles ahead of me. "We got places to go. People to see."

"Friends to keep upright," I said, hurrying after her.

Her walk wasn't as straight as normal, the sway in her saunter too obvious to go unnoticed. She had no reason to be behind the wheel of a car. She had even less reason to wander this party without someone watching her back.

We passed through clusters of people, humidity clinging to my bare arms and legs. A vintage Beatles tank top and blue jean cutoffs were trendy enough to fit in, but cool enough to spare me from the heat of the swamp. I absently rubbed my arms, eyeing people as the smell of burning pines carried on the breeze.

Ahead, a bonfire raged. Most of Crighton's junior and senior class stood gathered around the fire, red Solo cups in their hands.

"Want a drink?" Nikki said, glancing at me over her shoulder.

"How about a beer?" someone said from my right.

I glanced that way, eyeing Smith Saddler as he crossed a thick patch of brush with two beers in his hands. With jade-green eyes, perfectly styled brown hair, one heck of a saunter, and dark blue jeans, he was Crighton's closest thing to an athletic hipster. He carried the look well, and he knew it.

"Thanks!" Nikki said, taking a bottle from him. She put her lips to the rim, winking at me as she turned and headed the other way.

"She's drunk," I said, crossing my arms.

"Then I probably should've kept that beer," he said, grinning.

Smith's charm and overpowering stature were a recipe for trouble. He could talk his way out of a paper bag, then talk someone else into it.

"I texted Nikki earlier, asking about you," he said. "She didn't think you'd make it. Glad to see she was wrong."

I eyed him. His sharp jawline and broad shoulders were

carved to perfection, covered by a fitted button-down rolled at the sleeves. Too bad he was dangerous. One experience with a smooth talker was lesson enough.

"You probably should've been more worried about your wardrobe than whether or not I would be here," I said, grinning. "What's with this outfit, anyway? You look better suited for a photo shoot than a party."

"Um, the outfit wasn't my choice," he said, sipping his beer. "I had a meeting with college scouts earlier. Figured it was easier to head straight here, and get first shot at talking with you, than it would be to head into town, change, and try to steal you from another guy."

"You should've stopped to change."

"You should've gotten here earlier," he said.

He held the bottle out for me, but I declined.

"I'm not a beer girl, and I'm driving," I said, shaking my head. "Since Nikki pregamed with some kind of terrible vodka punch, I'd say it isn't even worth taking a sip. The likelihood of me having to carry her out of here in less than five minutes is ten to one."

"She was pregaming and didn't even invite me?!" he said, putting a hand to his chest. "With friends like those, who needs enemies?"

"With friends like those, I'll end up in a ditch," I said, shaking my head.

Smith paused, his lip tugging between his teeth. "Do you always jump to the worst-case scenario?"

"Not always," I said. "Sometimes I start off naive. That's usually when things end up the worst."

"Ah, so that's how you came up with that amazing cop car plan?" he said. "You started off naive, but somehow ended in the lake?"

"There was a little more to it than that," I said, glancing at the crowd.

"Like plotting how to get the keys, leaving it in neutral, and somehow jumping out of the car while it was moving?"

"If you want to paraphrase," I said.

Smith laughed, his gaze centered on me. "Most people want to believe Mitch was the mastermind, but I have my doubts. There's a little danger in that innocent face of yours."

"My face isn't innocent. I'm just—"

The breath left my lungs, burning away any coherent thought as Mitch left the tree line.

Tall and lean, with shaggy blond hair and casual clothes, he looked exactly like the guy who left Crighton too many months before. My gut churned with frustration. My brain refused to function.

"Speaking of Mitch," Smith said.

"Sorry," I said, tearing away my gaze.

Smith nodded and raked a hand through his hair. "Hey, I get the pair of you have a history. You don't have to apologize to anyone, especially me."

"I know," I said. "I was apologizing to myself, for even looking at him. He doesn't deserve the time."

"Truth."

In the distance, the shrill sound of multiple police sirens pierced the party like a needle through a balloon. Terror gripped my spine as red and blue lights flooded the space. *My dad.*

"Cops!" Smith yelled, dropping his bottle as he bolted for the trees.

I moved too, scrambling through the web of students.

"Alex!" I heard, the shrillness in Nikki's voice unmistakable.

I darted to the left, sprinting after her as she stumbled toward the cars.

The Prius's lights blinked to life as we bolted toward it. Tires slung muck everywhere, turning the flurry of cars into a muddy pool of speeding vehicles and flashing lights.

Nikki yanked open the driver's door, sliding inside as a car narrowly missed her hood.

I slammed the door, my pulse racing as Nikki floored the pedal. She spun out before I could even get my seat belt fastened, sliding through the mud after a cluster of vehicles ahead.

"Watch the cop!" I screamed, spotting one of my dad's deputies as he raced toward our car. Nikki narrowly missed him, swerving to the left and onto the road.

Adrenaline rushed through me as she floored a pothole, the unpaved road banging us into the windows and roof.

"Hurry!" I said, staring out the back window.

Red and blue lights were following us, flashing shadows on the long line of trees spanning the sides of the road.

"I'm going!" she screamed, yanking hard on the wheel as we closed in on the shoulder.

I turned back around, blood rushing my face as two pairs of red lights blared at us through the front windshield. They were close. Too close.

"Nikki!" I said, sinking back into the seats when she didn't dodge them.

The impact shot me immediately against the dash.

Pain racked its way through my body, spinning a weightless web of darkness as a blaring horn shifted into a dull hum. The taste of copper grew thick on my tongue. My eyes refused to open.

Slowly, everything shifted into darkness. Silence overwhelming.

Then, nothing remained.

1

Feelings

"And that's the story of how I almost died," I said, leaning back in an oversized chair.

Dr. Heichman looked at me over a pair of wire-rimmed glasses. The literal embodiment of every old-school psychologist, the guy's expression had barely shifted from neutral to annoyed. At least my parents gave me a reaction whenever they wanted to talk about the accident.

"Are we done?" I said, turning my attention toward a window. "Or can we at least move on to something less exciting and more important, like, I don't know: how and why there's a horrible Rembrandt knockoff hung on this wall? At least try to find a painter people won't recognize. This one is terrible."

"Not all of my clients are as interested in art as you," he said.

"Guess I'm the special one."

Dr. Heichman lowered his pen and closed his notebook. "We

could spend the rest of your session discussing the qualities that are truly a reflection of your uniqueness, or we could focus on why you recount the car accident in such an unattached fashion."

"You asked me to talk about it," I said, staring at him. "I gave you a play-by-play for the millionth time. It is what it is."

"True. You can't change what happened."

"Then why are we still talking about it?" I said. "We've been talking about it for, I don't know, six months."

"Because I've been at this long enough to know when a client is burying their feelings and refusing to acknowledge the implications of something as traumatic as the death of a friend," he said.

Breath hung in my chest, suffocating.

"Well, I think I've managed just fine," I said after a pause. "Maybe I don't have to grieve the way you think I should."

"Okay. How do *you* think you should be grieving?"

I shifted in the chair, my fingernails digging into the fine leather armrests. Conversations about this were like a nick in my Achilles tendon. Destructive. Painful.

I swallowed, facing the window again.

"You can't keep your emotions bottled in," he said, his voice like sandpaper. "That's like funneling helium into a balloon until it reaches full capacity. You need to release the pressure before it pops; let out some of the tension and slowly adjust. If you don't, you'll break."

"I already broke," I said, blinking at him. "My friend died. High school went down the drain. Now here I am, stuck in an office with you while you tell me how I should and shouldn't handle my grief."

"Being abrasive is completely understandable."

"This isn't abrasive," I said, standing. "This is me." I grabbed my complimentary water bottle from the coffee table and crossed the room. "We're done for today."

"Sit down, Alex."

I shot him a peace sign over my shoulder and headed for the door.

"Alex."

I closed the door behind me, my sandals flip-flopping against polished tile floors as I headed for the lobby. Inside, my mom sat reading a copy of *Good Housekeeping*. I crossed the threshold, earning her attention as I closed the door.

"Well, that was quick," my mom said, closing the magazine.

"What can I say? He was on a roll today."

She stood and slung her purse over her shoulder, following me as she eyed her watch.

Our Thursday routine of afternoon therapy sessions started the previous November. With seven months of physical therapy finished and a Thursday time slot open for Dr. Heichman, Therapy Thursdays were our new norm.

Outside, late afternoon heat wrapped itself like a blanket around my skin. The lights on my mom's Equinox flashed, the car humming to life as we neared.

"We're meeting your father for dinner tonight," she said as I reached the passenger side. "He got off early. Thought crawfish étouffée sounded good."

"Yay for family dinners," I said, yanking open the door.

Having dinners with the both of them was like doing a swan dive into shark-infested waters. You had to watch your back or one of them would take a bite out of you before you realized they were there.

"So, did you and Dr. Heichman have a good visit?" my mom said a minute later. She pulled the car onto the street, adjusting the volume on the radio to a conversational level. "You got out fifteen minutes early. I don't want to make assumptions here—"

"Then don't."

"—but every time you get out early it's because he's hit on something you don't like. Was it the wreck again?"

"It's always the wreck," I said, settling my attention on the buildings outside. "That's why you signed me up for sessions with him, remember? That's what we talk about."

"We signed you up for sessions so you would have someone to talk to," she said.

"And a therapy app on my phone wouldn't do the job?" I said, glancing at her. She stared at me, expressionless. "I'll take that as a *no*."

"Apps aren't the same thing as a doctor, Alex. Besides, I like having you there in front of someone. It lets me know you aren't fiddling with other things while someone is trying to talk to you."

"Wrong. I'm always mentally fiddling with something. Today, for example, I was thinking about all the great knockoff paintings I've seen in my life and how crappy the one in his office is in comparison. I mean, he's rich enough to buy a decent one."

"That's what you do in there?"

"I also watch him write notes about me," I said, shrugging. "He has this notebook. It's huge. But he probably sends you the copies, so I'm sure you already know that."

"Wrong. Him sending me copies of anything would breach doctor-patient confidentiality," she said.

"Ah! I forgot. Those rules changed when I turned eighteen."

"Along with your voting status and your insurance premium," she said.

"Funny how things seem to shift as people get older," I said, raking overgrown bangs behind my ears. "Ooh, I bet curfew changes too. As in, there isn't any."

"As long as you live in our house, you abide by our rules," she said.

"I can fix that."

"You can't," she said, turning onto another road. "You have one more year in Crighton. You're stuck with us."

"Or I could just *not* get my diploma."

She glanced at me over the console, her lips a thin line. Conversations about graduation were her sensitive subject. It was either graduate or get cut off. She didn't care that the last part of my junior year was spent in the hospital. No. Make the eighteen-year-old go another year. Make your daughter the rainbow fish in a small bowl of crabs.

"Don't start that conversation," she said.

"It's called freedom, Mom. Get on board or get over it."

She rolled her eyes, an exasperated sigh passing her lips. "You're always like this after therapy."

"What? I happen to think I'm being nice," I said.

A cell phone rang through her car speakers. My dad's name flashed across the radio console.

"Deputy Doom," I said, wiggling my fingers at the screen.

"Hi, Jim," she said into the speaker, ignoring me.

"You two already out?" my dad answered.

"Yeah," my mom said. "Your daughter decided to end the session early, again. We should be there in five."

"She ended it early? Why? He charges too much money to skimp on any minutes."

"I wasn't interested in the conversation topic," I said.

"I don't know why we keep paying him all that money when all she does is waste that poor man's time," my dad said.

"I don't waste his time," I said, straightening. "I just choose what I do and don't want to talk about. It's called being independent. Making my own choices."

"He's the most prestigious therapist in Shreveport!"

"No number of flashy certificates and awards can handle me," I said. "If Dr. Pain in the Rear wants to help me navigate my feelings, he needs to figure out a better way to do it."

"Oh, Lord," he said through the speaker. "If he can't get to her, Loraine doesn't stand a chance."

"Loraine?" I said, staring at the radio.

My aunt, who I hadn't seen in years, was rarely talked about. She kept to herself in the backwoods of Texas, while we stayed in our quiet little corner of Louisiana. It worked, usually.

"That was random," I said, looking at my mom.

"Random how?" my dad said.

"I haven't gotten to that part of the conversation with her yet, Jim," my mom said, switching the call from hands-free to her cell phone.

"But now that it's been brought up and you're acting super shady, why don't you go ahead and continue with that conversation?" I said, shifting in my seat.

My mom glanced at me in her peripheral, her brow furrowed as she intentionally moved the phone to the left side of her face.

"No. No. I will," she said after a pause. "I was just waiting until we had a confirmation on her assignment. Was it cleared?"

"Was what cleared?" I said, looking at her.

She held a hand up but I batted it away, clutching the *oh crap* handle as the car shifted slightly. I surveyed the right of me, my pulse racing as I searched for cars in our blind-spot. Clear. Everything was clear.

"That's fine with me. Might be a bit challenging, but I'll take it," my mom said, slowing at a stoplight.

"Take what?" I said.

She held a hand up again, but my hand was safe and secure on the handle. Cars made me nervous. Swerving even more so.

"Okay. We're coming up on Ellie's now," she said, navigating downtown Shreveport. "Don't worry. I'll get it out of the way, in case she makes a scene."

"Scene? What scene?" I said, staring at her wide-eyed as she ended the call. "Like the screaming, crying, fighting kind, or the *I'm going to break a vase in your face* kind?"

"The second one sounds pretty vicious," she said, slowing into a parking space.

"Mom, what kind of scene?" I said.

"Before I say anything, I want you to promise to let me explain everything to you before you make any assumptions."

"Started every terrible conversation ever," I said, pinching the bridge of my nose.

"I wouldn't say it's terrible."

"Let me be the judge."

"Fine." She put the car in park, turning so her back was to the door. "Your dad and I have arranged for you to attend Loraine's summer camp."

Images of a hokey campground filled my brain. Loraine's delinquent camp for troubled youth was three hundred miles away. In Texas. In the heat. Negative. Not happening.

"I'm not going to Loraine's," I said, laughing. "But funny joke. Great job."

"It's summer camp or boarding school," she said. "Take your pick."

Spit caught in my throat, choking the life from me. *Boarding school?! Hold up. Was she serious?*

I checked the back seat for cameras, then stared at my mom again when I realized it wasn't a hidden camera game show. "Hang on. You really just said boarding school, didn't you?"

"We would prefer camp."

"Uh-uh," I said, holding my hands up. "I'm sorry, but the last time I checked this was a free country and I'm legally an adult. I pick option C. Neither."

"You have a college fund that might convince you otherwise," she said.

My face warmed. That college fund was mine to do whatever I wanted. If I went to school, great. If I took a gap year and explored all the artwork in Europe, great. All I had to do was graduate.

"We've been saving for you for college since you were a baby," she said. "But I speak for your father and me both when I say we're concerned about whether or not you'll be able to buckle down and focus on school the way you should focus on it. Your absences weren't the only thing that held you back, Alex. Your grades were abysmal. You're repeating your senior year more for that than anything."

Anger snaked its way up my spine, and I balled my fists against my legs. "Okay. The last time I checked, government and economics wasn't worth being high on my priorities list," I said. "I was focused on getting out of PT. You know, trying to be the girl who almost died. And now you want to sit here and give me some crappy ultimatum? That's messed up! That's *my* money."

"It's ours until we think you're fit enough to handle it," she said, shaking her head.

Red flooded my vision. "This is your way of getting revenge, huh?" I said, narrowing my eyes. "I tarnished your glowing reputation. Now you're forcing me into stupid therapy sessions, while stealing my money and shipping me off to camp! What kind of parents are you?!"

"I couldn't care less about my reputation," she said, looking at me with an unreadable expression that boiled my blood. "What I care about is you. I care about you throwing your life away. I care about you failing to see all the positives going for you, because you're too wrapped up in what happened last year.

"I genuinely hate the idea of you being that far from us. I hate the thought of something happening to you while you're there. But don't make me fight you on this. I don't want to fight you when I feel like I've spent the last year fighting a battle trying to save you from yourself."

Her words sliced me like a knife, shredding my heart and biting through any attempt I could muster at being difficult or distant. Overbearing or not, at least she cared.

"Then maybe you should quit trying to save me and let me save myself," I said.

Silence buried its way between us, a suffocating silence

turning my anxiety on overdrive. I bit my lip until blood tasted copper against my tongue, a mountain of terrible words battling the few pieces of sympathy I had left.

"If I go, I can't promise I'll come back."

"If you want this money, you will."

2

Welcome to Texas

"Ladies and gentlemen, welcome to Houston," the pilot said, "where it's a stifling one hundred and one degrees and eighty-three percent humidity. Local time, two thirty. We'll be taxiing for a minute."

"Which translates to: Congrats, you're about to melt your makeup off," I said, switching my iPhone off airplane mode.

Minutes later, the flight attendants opened the plane door. People rushed to stand, more eager to enter the world of impeding heat exhaustion than me. I waited until the aisle was clear, then yanked my duffel out of the overhead compartment and exited the plane.

Surprisingly, what I expected to be some cowboy-infested airport turned out to be a tech haven for waiting passengers. People sat around long tables at the terminals, propped on tall stools with a number of airport-provided tablets in front of them. Overhead, different signs and decorations littered the ceiling. Restaurants were at every angle, sandwiching gift shops and stores lining the walls.

"Fancy," I said, passing them en route for the baggage claim.

Ahead of me, a guy entered the escalator to the main floor. I sped up, eyeing his broad shoulders, towering height, sharp facial features, and eyes shadowed by the brim of a baseball cap.

"Maybe Texas isn't all bad," I said, watching him as I took my place on one of the steps.

We reached the baggage claim seconds later, him walking at a relaxed pace while I casually navigated the crowd to ensure prime position beside him. When I stopped at his right, his perfectly curved lips shifted into a smile.

Hello there.

The conveyor started, stealing his attention as bags started dropping. He passed me toward the conveyor, his arms flexing as he hauled a cardinal-blue suitcase to the ground.

My suitcase dropped two seconds later, hard-backed and black. I moved toward it and hauled it from the conveyor with a less impressive *hmph*.

"Alex!"

I turned in an instant, cringing as Loraine maneuvered through the crowd behind me. In a perfect world, she would've arrived ten minutes later and I could've *accidentally* run into the hot guy with my pretend runaway suitcase.

Her salt-and-pepper hair was in a ponytail at the crown of her head, her turquoise-colored Camp Kenton shirt setting off the bright red tinge in her sunburned cheeks. From the looks of it, she was in full summer mode. At least she wasn't dressed like a cowgirl.

She stopped in front of me, deep-set wrinkles around her eyes and mouth deepening as she grinned. "Welcome to Texas! I'm so excited you're here!"

She pulled me into a hug, the smell of sunblock and sweat thick on her skin.

"Thanks," I said, unpeeling myself before it drenched my clothes. I straightened the hem of my shirt, my fingers tightening around the suitcase handle.

"There you are!"

I narrowly dodged the barreling male who rushed her next. The hot guy hugged her tight, lifting her off the ground as she laughed out loud.

What is life?

"Thanks again for driving up here," he said, setting her down. "I owe you."

"You sure do!" she said, hands on her hips. "Nothing compares to rush-hour traffic!"

"Wouldn't be summer if I wasn't late to something," he said, grinning.

She smiled back, motioning at me now. "Truthfully, it wasn't all that inconvenient to pick you up. Had to get this one too. Can't make her walk all the way to camp, and they don't Uber that far."

"Surprised you know what an Uber is," he said, and his hazel eyes shifted my way. "Grant Carraway. It's nice to meet you."

"Alex Reynolds," I said, taking his hand. *Future wife.*

Grant's calloused fingers wrapped around mine in a firm shake, his dimpled smile drawing my attention. He was too good-looking to focus on anything else. This summer was definitely looking up.

"Alex is my niece," Loraine said beside me, taking my suitcase. "Our newest addition."

"Newbie," he said. "That means you get all the crappy jobs."

"Hey! Don't scare her off before I even get her out of the airport," Loraine said. She turned, heading for the doors. "I'm short-staffed as it is."

I scrunched my nose and followed behind them. Their conversation about random camp things was far less important than the quality of Grant's back muscles. How someone made a plain T-shirt look so good was pure magic.

Inside the parking garage, soul-crushing heat created an outdoor oven. Loraine motioned to a white four-door Chevy, stopping behind it as the taillights flashed to life.

"So, I was thinking it might be better to have rotating shifts this year," she was saying when Grant stopped beside her. "That way each counselor has a night off."

"I vote yes," he said.

"Okay. That's one vote. What do you think, Alex? Yes or no?"

"Huh?" I said, cocking my head to the side. Grant's impressive calf muscles and tantalizing backside were the only part of the walk to the truck I cared about.

"We're talking about nights off," she said, smiling. "Camp usually runs one two-month-long session. Do you think we should give staff members a weekly night off, or give them two nights off every second week?"

"Oh, um, whatever you think," I said, watching Grant lower the tailgate. He lifted my suitcase with ease, dropping it into the bed of the truck before grabbing his own.

"Which translates to weekly," he said, looking at Loraine.

"Not sure I heard those words come out of her mouth, but sure," Loraine said, walking to the driver's side.

I headed toward the passenger side, sliding onto scorching leather seats that burned the backs of my legs. Closing my eyes, I sucked in a shaky inhale and released it in one long breath.

Loraine's been driving for years. It's like my mom driving. I'm fine.

Dr. Heichman hadn't been able to get much out of me, but I didn't need him to know what triggered reactions and what didn't. New cars. New drivers. Unknown roads. Speeding. Anything resembling danger set my nerves on fire.

Grant slid into the back of the truck a few minutes later, his knees knocking against my seat. I scooted it up farther, putting my purse on my lap as I gauged the distance between me and the dash.

"All right," Loraine said, climbing into the driver's seat. "Music requests?"

"Nope," Grant and I said in unison, his tone substantially deeper than mine.

We merged onto I-45 a few miles later, Houston's scenery drowned by banjo-ridden classic country blaring from the radio. *I should've made a request.*

I slumped my head against the window, watching towns roll by while trying to ignore the terrible twang of some old-school country singer rambling about his love. It wasn't until we passed the massive Sam Houston statue outside Huntsville that I couldn't take it anymore. I adjusted the knob, glancing at my aunt over the console.

"So, what job have you and my parents decided to stick me

with?" I said. "Resident janitor? Pool girl? Arts and crafts guru who does nothing but paint all day?"

"If I put you in arts and crafts all day, I would be wasting your amazing people skills and sparkling personality," Loraine said.

"You clearly don't know me," I groaned.

"But I know and trust your parents, which is why I've decided to make you the counselor for girls' cabin two," she said. "Grant is your co-counselor. He can show you the ropes."

Dread and excitement mixed, churning something similar to nausea in the base of my stomach.

"We currently have the girls' side at full capacity," she said, looking at me. "There are two spots open on Grant's side, but I'm ninety percent sure those spaces will fill before camp starts. We still have a few days."

Grant pulled a pair of earbuds from his ears for the first time and leaned forward. His face hovered over the console, his brows pulled together in a deep V. "What is up? Are you talking to me?" he said, staring at her.

"More to Alex, though it does pertain to you," Loraine said, staring at him. "Cliffs Notes version: This is your co-counselor. Her side of the cabin is full. Your side will probably be full. I'll expect you to show her the ins and outs, while I'm trying to finish prepping for camper arrival."

Grant's jaw tightened. Had it not been for a staggering fear of death by car, I might have stayed more focused on his jaw.

"Not trying to offend anyone," he said slowly, "but don't you think Alex would be better off in one of the younger cabins? I mean, has she ever been a counselor before?"

"No, but I've gone to one," I said.

His brow furrowed. "Loraine," he said, shaking his head.

"What?" she said, smiling at him in the rear-view mirror. Loraine drifted onto a rumble strip, and I cringed.

"Putting her with you seemed like my best option," she said. "You've been around the longest. You know the rules like the back of your hand."

"And I'm arguably the most impatient counselor on your staff," he said. "I know I seem cool and shiny because I'm the counselor OG, but put her with Linc. He'll be much more equipped to answer her questions and deal with stupid things like camp tours and debriefings."

"Camp tours?" I groaned.

"I already put Linc with Kira," Loraine said, shaking her head. "Besides, I have full confidence you'll be the leader I know you are and will help her manage those campers to the best of her ability. Linc is a great counselor, but he lacks structure. She needs structure."

"She needs for you to not talk about her like she isn't here," I said, crossing my arms. I glanced over the console, staring at Grant. "For what it's worth, I'm totally down to just skip all the stupid *welcome to camp* stuff. I don't need a rundown on the rules. I don't need much of anything except the Wi-Fi password and the location of the nearest Starbucks."

"We passed the nearest Starbucks five minutes ago," Loraine said. "Also, the Wi-Fi password is solely for office use. We unplug while we're at camp. It helps keep campers and counselors dialed in to why they're there."

"I'm starting a petition," I said.

"Great. Focus on the petition and I'll focus on how to get you transferred to a better-suited cabin," Grant said, giving me a thumbs-up.

"Nothing is changing," Loraine said.

"Yet." He slumped into his seat, returning his earbuds to his ears.

I stared at the road the rest of the ride, impossible options burning their way through my brain. No amount of money was worth depriving myself of Starbucks. A sneak out would be imminent. Crucial to survival.

An hour later, a random Hank Wilson song was floating through the speakers when Camp Kenton's massive wood sign greeted us. Loraine turned beside it, driving through a pair of metal gates at the entrance.

I checked my phone reception, praying for a signal.

No service.

"Damn," I grumbled, cramming the phone in my pocket.

"AT&T is spotty out here," Loraine said, glancing at me. "You're welcome to use the office phone if you need to make a call."

"We've gone back in time, where internet and cell phones don't exist," I said. "What's next? We park the car and go the rest of the way on foot?"

"Nah. The camp has its own covered wagon," Grant said, unbuckling his seat belt.

I surveyed him, gauging his seriousness as we neared a portable building with CAMP OFFICE painted on the side. A large metal sign hung in front of it. A single golf cart was the only vehicle in sight.

Loraine parked on the other side of the golf cart, pulling

the key from the ignition and quickly opening the driver's side door. Heat flooded the cab, amplifying warmth in my cheeks as I watched Grant unfold himself from the back of the truck. His long arms stretched above his head, revealing a sliver of skin. He was more distracting than Wi-Fi.

I slipped outside the truck, surveying the scenery as I closed the door. Trees extended in every direction, shading long patches of freshly mowed grass. My new prison was a virtual greenhouse, the canopy of leaves magnifying the stifling heat.

"Hey," Grant said, earning Loraine's attention. "I'm hungry. Is there any chance I could skip unpacking and get straight to the food?"

"Mess hall," she said, nodding. "I think Subway sandwiches were on the lunch menu. If you're lucky, Phil might have saved you some chicken salad."

"My favorite," Grant said, grinning.

Loraine crossed the grass toward the camp office, leaving me with Grant and zero idea of where to go next.

"You interested in food, or are you still over there trying to mentally plan your petition?" he said.

"You volunteering to be my first signature?"

"If it gets me out of the chaperone gig, then yes," he said, fidgeting with the brim of his baseball cap. He shifted his weight, eyes assessing me beneath its shadow.

"You can stop giving me the judgy look," I said, moving to my right. "I know I'm not Grade A counselor material."

"Not even close," he said, scrunching his nose.

I gawked, shooting an equally assessing gaze at him. "For the record, you don't strike me as counselor of the year either. You look like some athletic hipster crossbreed with perfect hair and a perfect face, who would run at the first sign of chaos."

"I'm not even remotely close to being a hipster," he said, "and I thrive in chaos. My middle name is *chaos*."

I arched a brow.

"Okay, it's Michael, but that's not the point. Point is: You're horrible at reading people. These campers are going to chew you up and spit you out."

"Wrong." *Except he was probably mostly right.*

"Then I'll happily take all my *wrong* personality assessments of you with me to the mess hall. You can find the way on your own. Don't want to continue misjudging you and your expert people-reading skills."

"Your sarcasm could use some work," I said, hurrying after him.

After a few steps, we reached a concrete sidewalk leading to a massive cabin down the way. Grant paused, waving at the group on its large wraparound porch. "This is the counselor cabin," he said, nodding toward the building. "And those are more judgy counselors like myself. Do you want to meet them while you're hangry, or would you prefer to meet them after a sandwich or two?"

"I never said I was hangry."

"It's in your eyes," he said, winking.

I let out a long sigh, my grumbling stomach confirming my appetite. The small sandwich I'd scarfed between my house and Shreveport's airport had barely made a dent.

"What if I'm not comfortable going strange places with strange people?" I said.

"I asked myself that exact same question, yet here I am staring at you."

I mentally flipped him off as he continued walking, his long legs increasing the distance between us. I jogged to catch up, huffing at the humidity clinging to my lungs.

"At the risk of sounding whiny, could you walk any slower?" I said, swatting away a cloud of mosquitoes.

"No," he said, glancing at me over his shoulder. "There's too much ground to cover between here and the mess hall. Besides, you aren't the only one who's hungry. If you don't like the pace, I can bring you a sandwich if and when I eventually grab my bags."

"How long might that be?" I said.

"An hour. Five hours. Who knows? Depends on who I run into and how much time I can spend stalling before Loraine assigns me to showing you around some more."

"Hey, I already said I didn't need a tour," I said, catching up with him. "I don't really need or want to be a counselor either."

"Great! Then refuse to do it and let her hook me up with a co-counselor who will actually pull her weight."

"I'm stronger than I look."

"I didn't mean literal weight," he said, pausing. He surveyed me, his lips pursed.

"You were kidding, right?" he said after a minute.

"Maybe. Maybe not," I said, walking again.

Ahead, six smaller cabins came into view. Three lined one side of the road while the remaining three lined the other side.

Grant pointed at them. "That's where we'll be staying. Cabins one, two, and three are on the left. Four, five, and six are on the right. We're in two, which means we're right there in the middle."

I eyed cabin two, frowning. Like a miniature version of the counselor cabin, this cabin also had a tin roof and wraparound porch. The main difference was two doors on its exterior—one on the right side of the porch and one on the left. A large metal 2 separated them, identifying the building.

"You and your group will be on the right. Me and my group will be on the left," he said. "Both groups have their own cots, showers, et cetera. They're basically the exact same floor plans, except I think your side is maybe one or two feet bigger."

"Nifty."

"Yeah," he said. "Back in the day, campers had to sleep on concrete slabs with tarps as a makeshift cover. It was legit camping, but it sucked. Anytime a tornado or other serious storm system rolled through, everyone had to pack up and move to the mess hall."

"Nothing says safe haven like someone getting sucked into a tornado," I said.

Grant chuckled, walking toward the set of cabins on the opposite side of the road. Trees were thicker behind them, hiding a dirt path that twined its way through.

"The pool is down that path," he said, pointing at it. "Maybe a quarter mile or so. Are you lifeguard certified?"

"Nope."

"CPR certified?"

"Nope."

"Nature enthusiast?"

"No," I said, hands on my hips. "I literally hate nature with a burning passion. I mean, I love Earth, but I'm a city girl through and through."

"Fantastic! That's exactly what I want to hear when I'm showing my *co-counselor* around the largest summer camp this side of Lufkin." He crossed his arms and shook his head. "You do realize you'll be out here for two months, right? With little to no interaction with anything city related?"

"You know, I do remember Loraine saying something about no Starbucks and no Wi-Fi. Maybe I dreamed that conversation but—"

"At least your personality kind of makes up for your lack of qualifications," he said.

"You haven't even seen the best parts," I said.

He rocked back on his heels, letting out a low whistle. "Attitude."

"Hungry and annoyed," I said, shrugging.

"Default setting?"

"Only when my tour guide has decided to keep me from food in favor of flirting with me," I said. "Which I'm assuming is why you've quit walking."

"I quit walking because I'm one of those guys who has a hard time explaining things to people while simultaneously trying to work out situations in his brain."

"Enlighten me."

"Okay," he said. "Riddle me why your aunt decided to give you a counselor position when she could've easily put you in some basic office job."

"I don't know. Ask her."

"I'm asking you," he said.

"Well, you're asking the wrong person, because I literally have no answers for you. I got the info the same time as you. Got the same explanation. Your questions are exactly the same as mine. Trust me, I would've been cool with some basic job. I don't want to be a counselor."

"Then don't be," he said. "Let someone who's capable of doing the job have it."

"Oh, so I'm incapable?"

"Aren't you?"

I sucked in a breath. *Yes. But that didn't mean I wanted it pointed out.*

"That was rude," I said.

"I'm just repeating what you've pretty much said," he said. I shot him a narrowed gaze and he chuckled. "Okay, let's recap. You're unqualified. Yes or no?"

"Technically."

"And you don't want to be a counselor?"

"Correct."

"And you hate nature?"

"That's what I said."

"Then you're completely incapable of doing this job!" he said, grinning. "I mean, let's be real. You walked in here and got handed a job most of us had to *earn*. That, in and of itself, should be a huge red flag in your capability rating. You've even said you don't want this job. Me calling you incapable isn't remotely rude."

"It was," I said, rolling my eyes.

"Because you've decided to be suddenly sensitive about it," he said, raising a hand to the brim of his hat.

"I'm not being sensitive. I'm just . . . I'm hungry and this trek to the mess hall has somehow shifted from a camp tour to a conversation about what I am and am not capable of. Not that you have any right to voice your opinion," I said. "You've known me all of a car ride and here you are explaining to me why I'm *incapable* of being a counselor."

"I'm just saying there are counselor candidates out here that are far more qualified than you," he said. "The campers will need someone who wants to be out here, who wants to be around them. If you don't have the patience or knowledge to do that job, you're pretty much asking for failure. And, not to come across as an even bigger asshole than you seem to think I am, but I can't babysit someone grossly underqualified while trying to balance my own duties as a counselor. That's impossible."

"No one's asking you to babysit me," I said, crossing my arms.

"That's exactly what she's doing!"

There was an irritation in his tone that wasn't there before. It set my nerves on edge, raising a wall between me and any words he could hurl my way.

"I'm not trying to be the bad guy by telling you the truth, but being a counselor is hard. It's real hard. You wouldn't last a day."

"You want to bet on it?" I said.

"You'll quit day one," he said, nodding.

"Deal." I brushed past him, intentionally jamming my shoulder into his. The action was less climactic than expected. His muscles hit my arm like a rock-solid door with a padlock.

"The food is that way," he said, his voice behind me as I kept walking.

"I'll get some later. You ruined my appetite."

I followed the path, aiming for a semi-dramatic exit. Grant could judge me all he wanted, but I never made a bet I couldn't keep. I would survive day one, and I would do it smiling.

3

Personality

"Or I'll die in the woods on day one," I said, glancing at the poorly marked map I'd swiped from Loraine's office.

The goal was to give myself my own camp tour, since Grant's was such a huge failure. But even my stubbornness couldn't match Camp Kenton's woods. After an hour of wandering aimlessly, I plopped to the earth with a sigh.

"She survived an accident but somehow managed to die in the woods," I said, leaning against a tree. "Here lies Alex Reynolds, the girl who couldn't read a map."

I blinked tired eyes to the woods, my shirt clinging to my body like a wet rag. Humidity had soaked the hair on my neck hours before. My bangs now clung to my forehead, beads of sweat rolling into my eyes and down my cheeks. I pushed them to the side, mud forming on my fingers.

Beside me, a spider worked its way over the leaves. I kicked at it, my sandals doing little to protect my feet from twigs and mud. If this was what the bottom of the barrel looked like, its loneliness was severely underrated.

Trees limbs crunched behind me, the rattle of leaves sending me full circle. Grant crossed through them, scowling as he came to a stop. "Like I said, you're incapable. It's nothing personal. It's fact."

He handed me a water bottle, condensation clinging to the plastic. I took it, my flushed cheeks and dehydrated body begging for relief.

"Can we go now?" he said. "I've got a mile-wide list of things to do, and I can't sit in these woods with you while you pout and play in the dirt. I've done that long enough. Responsibility calls."

I swallowed hard, dragging the rim from my lips. "What do you mean you've done this long enough?" I said, my grip on the bottle tightening. "How long have you been here?"

"Long enough to know you aren't capable of finding your way back alone," he said, sweat around the ring of his collar evidence enough. "And long enough to know you need a serious lesson on how to read a map."

"The person who made the map did a crappy job," I said, standing.

"*I* made the map. It's the handler who did the crappy job. Not the mapmaker."

Grant turned, pushing a branch out of his way as he walked. "How did you even get to this part of the woods?" he said. "I swear, it's like you searched for the most snake-ridden area, then decided to sit down right in the middle of it. You know what a rattlesnake is, don't you?"

"Yes," I said. "They rattle."

"Among other things, like biting you."

"I'll take my chances," I said, trying to keep Grant's pace.

When we reached the edge of the woods, the sun was hovering over the horizon. Grant turned, frustration flickering over his face until it neutralized to something unreadable.

"Head to the counselor cabin near the camp office," he said.

"Is that an order?"

"No. It was a request," he said, rolling his eyes. He let out a long breath and turned the opposite way, taking long strides through the grass. "I'll be there in a minute. I need to do something first."

"Like find a clean shirt?" I said, turning the opposite way.

"It would be clean if I didn't have to stalk you all over the woods," he said behind me.

I trekked the dirt path, heading toward the counselor cabin. When I passed, a group of counselors gathered on cabin one's porch eyed me quietly. My muddy, sweaty, mosquito-eaten appearance had to make one heck of a first impression. *Hello. I'm the swamp thing. Nice to meet you.*

Near the camp office, the counselor cabin's porch was vacant. I took its steps one at a time, crossing the creaky wooden planks toward the door at the front. Inside the cabin, the air conditioner's chill mixed with the dampness of my shirt. I rubbed my arms; goose bumps covered my skin as I walked the wood floor.

A navy-and-white plaid couch sat in the middle of the living room. Worn cushions and frayed edges on the arm gave it an aged feel. I plopped onto it, grabbing one of two plaid pillows tossed haphazardly on the cushion. Grant entered a few minutes later, the screen door closing loudly behind him.

"I half expected to show up and find out you'd gone to the wrong cabin," he said, tossing a granola bar at me. "At least you paid attention to something other than my backside."

"It was only temporary," I said, holding my ground despite heat flooding my cheeks. He wasn't wrong.

He chuckled, plopping into the chair across from me. "At least Loraine paired me up with someone with a sense of humor. I'll give her credit for that."

"That was nice," I said, looking at him.

"Nice enough for you to request a job change?"

"A bet is a bet," I said, scratching my arms.

Littered with red splotches from all the mosquito bites, keeping that bet would be even harder now. These stupid mosquitoes were like tiny raptors bent on destroying my happiness.

"Quit scratching," he said, drawing my attention.

"They itch."

"You're in Texas at the beginning of June. What did you expect? Mosquitoes are our state bird."

His hat hit the table and messy strands of chestnut-colored hair poked out on either side of his head. His face, tanned from the sun, was somehow sharper without the shadow of his hat. He raked his hands through his hair, smoothing the strands against his forehead.

"What possessed you to go out there anyway?" he said. "Did you just see the woods and think, *Wow, that looks like a great place to go*?"

"I was giving myself a camp tour, since you failed so epically at it earlier," I said.

"You could've stuck with something easy like touring the junction or finding the mess hall."

"I was trying to find the pavilion," I said. "It was the only thing not centrally located and, because it was stuck out in the woods, it seemed like the most challenging thing on the map."

"You like a challenge?"

"That's how I roll."

"Well, maybe you should think about slowing that roll," he said. "If it weren't for me, you'd be stuck out there all night, fending off snakes, brown recluses, and who knows what else. Maybe ghosts. Rumor round here is those woods are haunted."

"Ghosts don't scare me anymore," I said, relaxing into the couch.

Grant let out a deep breath and rested the back of his head against the chair, his eyes focused on the roof. He had a point. Had it not been for him finding me, I would have still been out there.

"Besides, maybe my intention was to get lost," I said, staring at him. "Maybe I wanted to spend an afternoon admiring the beauty of Camp Kenton's forest."

"I'm calling bull," he said, shaking his head. "You got yourself lost, then had to wait on someone to come and find you since you were too stubborn to ask me to show you around. I heard you rambling about how you thought you were going to die out there. Whatever happened to perseverance and effort? It was like you were content to sit out there and be miserable."

"I was tired and I'd already wandered the woods to the point where trying to find my way out was doing more harm than good," I said. "Get off me about it and focus on something productive, 'kay?"

"Still have that attitude, huh?"

"It's a permanent feature," I said. "You'll get used to it.

Besides, you were the one who made it a point to tell me I was incapable and undeserving of my position."

"Which ended up being true, since you decided to spend your day out in the woods instead of actually doing something productive." He eyed my face, his expression unreadable. "Look, I hate to be the bearer of bad news, but on top of all your other missing qualifications, you're currently the only counselor who hasn't set up her cabin. Congrats."

"Are you kidding me?" I groaned.

"Nope," he said. "That little adventure got you more behind than you already are."

"It wasn't an adventure. I was proving a point."

"That you could get lost?"

I scowled and nestled into the couch, ignoring the pair of hazel eyes staring at me from across the room. I could sleep now and move mountains in the morning. *How's that for an inspirational quote?*

"You would have been better off staying with me. I could have helped you find the beds. I could have helped you find the bedding for the beds. Heck, I could have helped you get the place cleaned up and bug free, but no. You decided to lose yourself in the woods. Epic fail."

I turned my head, narrowing my eyes at him. "You do realize you're stuck with me, don't you, and that a fail for me is a fail for cabin two?"

He smiled. "Oh, so now you want to be a team?"

"Isn't that what we're supposed to be?"

"It is," he said. "Except I think we can both agree that this *team* is probably going to be far from fifty-fifty. I'm going to be the one loaded down with responsibilities. You're going to be the one messing everything up and adding to that list of responsibilities. The writing is on the wall."

I laughed a little, biting back irritation sizzling in my blood. So confident. So fully mistaken on whom he was actually dealing with.

"All right," I said, sitting straighter. "Let's get one thing straight, Grant. I might be way out of my element here, but I don't put up with crap from people back home and I'm not putting up with it from you. I appreciate that you came and *rescued* me from the forest, because yeah that was an idiot move on my part, but don't get it twisted. It might take a minute, but I will get my footing here. When that happens, you had better get the hell out of my way or I'll run you over. 'Kay?"

He studied me, quiet intensity burning behind his hazel eyes. The look made my heart pound. Anger. Frustration. Attraction. Too many emotions playing at my nerves.

Either way, this summer had to work. Grant could play nice, or spend the rest of his summer in co-counselor hell. The choice was totally up to him.

I cleared my throat and pushed myself off the couch.

"Where you going?" he said.

"To work on *my* side of *our* cabin," I said, heading for the door. "Got to make sure we keep this thing fifty-fifty, right?"

"Absolutely," he said. "I look forward to seeing what you actually bring to this partnership."

"Personality," I said, crossing the threshold. "Since I'm the only one with it."

The screen door closed loudly behind me, late-afternoon heat warming my bones. I took the path to cabin two, passing counselors gathered on cabin one's porch. I was the uncool kid at the party, killing their conversation as soon as I was in earshot. Their murmurs stayed low until I crossed cabin two's porch. I pushed my way through the door on the right, immediately gagging as the putrid smell of must burned my nostrils.

"Oh. My. God," I said, pinching my nose as I stared at the dusty interior.

The room's wooden floors were covered in a thick layer of red dirt, looking like a broom hadn't been taken to them since 1985. In addition, the wall unit wasn't on, creating a blistering hot interior that clung to the stale scent with a steel grip. I gagged, doing a one-eighty in less than ten seconds.

"Never mind," I said, heaving in clean air. "I'll work on being fifty-fifty tomorrow."

In front of the cabin beside me, five strangers looked my way. I let out a hacking cough, ignoring them as Grant joined the group.

"Needs a little bit of work," he said, smiling. "I'll work on my personality. You work on that."

4

Disaster

No amount of luck could fix the disaster known as my side of cabin two.

As the sun faded into darkness, I surrendered to dirt and grime. I woke up the next morning with the sun peeking through the windows of the counselor cabin. Sleeping in cabin two, in its current state, was like asking to get sick. Not happening.

My neck ached from the worn-out couch cushions, my back from hours spent trying to scrub my side of cabin two. Against my better judgement, I attemped to fix my side of the cabin. Mistake number one million and three.

I stood, slowly, creeping across the counselor cabin's wooden floor to the bathroom, where I spent the next forty-five minutes trying to get ready.

Halfway through my makeup routine, a teenager with a patterned head wrap and a massive makeup bag stopped in front of the bathroom door. Her dark brow furrowed, her mouth splitting into a wide grin.

"So this is where you disappeared to!" she said, smiling. "I got here late last night and tried to catch you in your cabin. Didn't even think to look in here.

"Kira Davis," she said, extending her hand. "I apologize in advance for you being stuck with Grant. Loraine told me yesterday. He's my friend and all, but girl, I was more than happy to find out I got partnered with Linc instead."

"You mean I'm not the only one who finds him annoying?" I said, grinning.

"Uh, no. Ninety percent of the time he's a pain in the rear," she said, laughing. "He means well, but they don't make them much thicker headed than Grant. He comes by it naturally. You can't blame him for his genetics."

"So his parents are also stubborn, annoying, and lack a personality?"

"Kind of."

She leaned against the door frame, her brown eyes scanning me. "But, despite him being difficult, you should take Loraine pairing you with him as a compliment. She trusts you can handle yourself around him, or she would've paired you with someone else. Can't go losing more counselors this close to camp starting. That's asking for a disaster."

"More counselors?" I said.

"Yeah, the girl originally assigned to cabin five ended up getting a summer internship and had to pull out last minute. I got switched. You took my spot in cabin two. But I'm totally okay with it. I want to be an elementary school teacher, so it's not like I won't be around younger kids eventually."

I turned back toward the mirror, frowning. Why couldn't Loraine put *me* somewhere I could use my talents? Arts and crafts, for example. I could paint all day, instead of managing fourteen-year-olds.

"So, anyway," Kira said. "I came up here to use the bigger vanity mirror. Is it cool if I hang out while waiting my turn? Everyone else is already at breakfast. It's biscuits and gravy day, and I recently jumped on the gluten-free train. I'd rather use this time to prep for the day, then scout out the kitchen for some fruit later. Phil always gets me the hookups on produce. It's not like they'll be out."

"Phil sounds like someone I need to be friends with."

"He's the best," she said, grinning.

I swept a couple of coats of mascara across my lashes, then finished off my makeup with a little bit of blush. It did nothing to hide the four-inch scar, pale against my sunburned forehead, but A-plus for effort.

Kira eyed the scar. "I've got one of those," she said, shifting her gaze. "My mom calls them stories. I call them things I can cover with a little bit of creativity."

She motioned toward a compass tattoo inked beneath her elbow. The tattoo's dark shadows contrasted her mahogany skin, the lines and intricate elements accentuating a jagged line inked into an arrow. It was a true piece of art. She was lucky enough hers was where she could shape it into something valuable. Mine wasn't so easy to hide.

"This place in Austin did it during my freshman year of college," she said, looking at me again. "It's the best investment I've ever made."

"I would be totally down to cover mine up with a tattoo, but I don't think inking a four-inch tattoo on my forehead would be a great life choice," I said, scrunching my nose. "Some people can pull off a face tattoo. I'm not one of them."

"Then highlight that sucker to perfection," Kira said, shrugging.

"Or cover it with carefully placed bangs," I said, swooping my long bangs to the side. "The less I have to talk about it, the better."

"Noted," she said, straightening against the door frame.

"But don't let that keep you from hurling all those inspirational quotes my way," I said, smiling as I pulled my makeup bag from the counter. "I'll take friends with inspirational quotes over zero friends and total isolation, any day."

"Well, I'm here all summer," she said, nodding. "You need a pep talk, I'm your girl. If you're feeling unfriended, I'm your girl. Kira Davis, positivity on fleek."

"Got it," I said, giving her a thumbs-up. "And I will more than likely be hitting you up on that offer, since I still have to deal with Grant the rest of the summer."

"Only the strong survive," she said, half laughing.

My smile widened as I took one last look in the mirror. "We'll see how that theory holds up," I said, crossing the threshold. "If I'm still here by lunch, you'll know you were right."

"I have faith in you," Kira said, placing her makeup bag on the counter. "But if you need some backup, check cabin five. I'm not much of a fighter, but I've put Grant in his place a time or two."

"Good to know," I said, waving at her over my shoulder.

I hauled my makeup bag back into the living room and left it beside the couch, exiting the counselor cabin two seconds later. Outside the camp office, Loraine stood beside a tall metal bell. She heaved a piece of rope up and down, forcing it to clank loudly enough I had to cover my ears.

"They have an actual breakfast bell," I said, rolling my eyes.

I stepped off the porch, walking the concrete path until it shifted into the dirt road that ran in front of the cabins. Grant caught me as I passed the second one, wearing the same black baseball cap from the day before. He had traded out his old T-shirt for a gray one and was wearing black athletic shorts and tennis shoes different from the day before.

He matched my pace, smelling like cedarwood-and-cypress-blended body wash. Looking good and smelling like this was unfair to the human population.

"I see you opted out of sleeping in your cabin last night," he said, grinning. "I think that's a first for a counselor."

"According to you, I'm not like the other counselors," I said, continuing to walk. "Besides, I was worried sleeping in that cabin would leave me as dead-hearted as you."

"Witty."

"I'm a fairly witty person," I said, glancing at him. "It's one of my most prominent personality traits. I'd say it ranks up there with spiteful and vindictive."

"Did you forget to include overdramatic in this list?" he said, grinning. "If I remember correctly, that was a pretty prominent personality trait."

"I haven't had near enough caffeine needed to deal with you this early in the morning," I said, stopping. "Get to the point and get on your way. I'm hungry."

"I just wanted to ask how your cabin cleanout went," he said. "If you opted to spend the night in the counselor cabin, I'm guessing it didn't happen. On a scale of one to Dallas Cowboy football, how bad was it?"

"That's a stupid analogy," I said, rolling my eyes.

"Give me a minute and I can think of a better one."

"Do we really have to chat, though? Can we not and just say we did?"

"We could, but since we're stuck with each other, communication isn't exactly optional," he said, taking off a Texas Tech lanyard hanging around his neck. "We have to talk. Let's start with something small and easy to navigate."

He handed me the lanyard, then pulled a piece of paper from his pocket and handed it to me too.

"Those are your counselor keys," he said. "I figured you had nowhere to put them, so consider that a gift. Wreck 'em Tech."

"I need caffeine," I said, eyeing a calendar that included *Team Building Sessions 1–5*, *Group Therapy*, and *Yoga for the Soul*. "Are these optional activities?"

"Nope. That's our preassigned schedule, courtesy of Loraine," he said. "Check line three, on today. See the part where you're scheduled for counselor prep from nine to twelve?"

My stomach dropped.

"That lovely line means you're stuck with me for the better part of the morning," Grant said. "It also means I'm here for all your co-counselor needs."

"Where's the nearest cliff?" I said, handing it back.

"Just drink in the moment and reflect on how lucky you are to have me as a co-counselor," he said, cramming the paper in his pocket.

"I'd rather drink whiskey," I said, shaking my head.

We entered a part of camp I had visited only once the day

before. The mess hall sat at the end of it, its roof gleaming in the sunlight.

"Do you want a proper introduction to the junction?" Grant said, motioning at the freestanding buildings around us. "Or would you like to forgo the official camp tour, once and for all?"

"Is there anything I need to know about the junction?" I said, quirking a brow.

Architecturally, the buildings were different from the cookie-cutter cabins we were supposed to sleep in. Reflecting more of a western feel, their flat porches and solid exteriors were less lodge-looking and more rustic.

My brow furrowed as my eyes scanned their signs. MEDICINE AND MORE. THE HUT. OLD TOWNE OPRY.

"Not really," he said, walking ahead. "The buildings are pretty self-explanatory."

"Then I'll skip this part of the tour," I said.

We continued walking, nearing the mess hall at the end of the road. The metal-roofed building with large screened-in windows at the front, two benches outside, and a door on each end looked more like something concocted of Lincoln Logs. It was the perfect addition to the junction's buildings, totally camp chic.

Grant reached the door before me. The hinges creaked as he opened it, and the smell of biscuits was overpowering from the other side.

With its wood-paneled walls and iridescent lights, the mess hall looked like *school cafeteria goes to camp*. Boat oars hung on the walls, pictures scattered beneath them, while Camp Kenton's flags hung from the ceiling.

Large folding tables ran from wall to wall, sandwiched by

metal chairs. Grant bypassed the tables and headed straight for two serving lines on the other side. Counselors stood there, divvying biscuits and gravy onto their plates.

We reached them, my stomach growling as I grabbed a plate from the stack. Two minutes later, I left the line with a loaded-down plate of biscuits, gravy, eggs, and bacon. Grant walked ahead of me to the other side of the room, taking a chair at the longest table in the middle. I set my plate beside his, the metal chair scraping against the concrete floor. A few people looked my way. I forced a smile and sat down, nerves on end at the number of people in the room.

"Okay, agenda for today," Grant said, filling his glass with orange juice. "First things first, you need to meet the other counselors. I know I'm irresistibly charming, but you need friends other than me. Hard to believe, I know."

"Uh-huh, what am I really doing?" I said, scooping eggs onto my fork.

"Primarily getting your side of the cabin set up," he said, putting the pitcher of juice back on the table. "I'd consider you spending the night in the counselor cabin a complete cop-out of your responsibilities. Use today to get your cabin ready for campers. Show you're actually capable of your position."

"Don't start on me," I said, swallowing my food. "I have bigger things to worry about than your unneeded and inaccurate opinion of me."

"Ooh. Did I strike a nerve?"

"Don't kid yourself," I said. "I wouldn't give you the satisfaction of getting under my skin."

"Why are you acting like I don't bug you when you obviously know I do?" he said, grinning.

"Fine," I said, facing him. "You get on my nerves. There. Happy?"

"Slightly."

"I swear, it's like you get satisfaction out of making me miserable," I said, tightening my grip on the fork.

"I mean, you're not far off."

My blood simmered and my cheeks warmed with heat. "Is this how you are with campers too?" I said, my volume rising. "Those poor kids don't stand a chance with all your nagging."

"Hold up," he said. His body shifted toward me and the line in his jaw sharpened as he stared at me beneath the rim of his hat. "We can flirt, but if you're seriously questioning *my* ability as a counselor we have a problem. Don't piss me off."

"You spent yesterday telling me how incapable I am. Why would you get pissed off when I question your capability?" I said.

His jaw cocked to the side, and the intensity in his gaze was enough to make me slink back into my chair. "I'm the best counselor out here," he said slowly.

"Why? What made you the golden boy? Couldn't be your sympathy. Definitely couldn't be the way you make everyone feel so warm and welcome."

He paused. "I'm going to pretend this is your lack of caffeine talking."

"Oh, I'm wide-awake and fully-functioning," I said. "Me asking you a question has zero to do with whether or not I've had coffee. So, I'll ask you again: Why are you the best? Why has Loraine handpicked you to be her number one, when there are people like Kira who are actually warm and welcoming, and willing to make me feel something other than incapable?"

Grant cleared his throat, momentarily scanning the otherwise-quiet mess hall. When his attention resettled on me, a sense of calmness lay in his expression.

Goose bumps tingled their way across my skin and my heart slowed in my chest.

"I don't know, Alex. Maybe because I proved myself," he said, the edge in his tone harsher than I expected.

We weren't flirting anymore. This was something different. More serious.

"You don't know me," he said, still talking low. "So, you can sit over there and toss around all the scenarios you want, but at the end of the day, everyone who's been around me more than five seconds knows I earned my spot. They can't say that about you."

"Meaning?"

"You're nothing more than the camp director's privileged niece."

I slumped back into my chair, shock rattling its way through my body.

"You're entitled, out of your league, and in for a rude awakening. This isn't a game, Alex. It's a job."

He slid back the chair and grabbed his plate. The rest of the room was silent as the dead. My cheeks burned as he stalked away, and collective murmurs slowly started as he exited the mess hall.

For a guy so sure of himself, Grant ran at the first sign of pushback. Gold-star counselor or not, it was a flaw in his armor. If I was lucky, that would be all the leverage I would need.

5

Sensitivity

Three hours later, sweat dripped down the back of my neck. I moved across the semi-clean floor of cabin two, glancing at dust-covered cobwebs scattered along exposed beams overhead.

The windowsills, however, were cobweb-free, and the windows were open, welcoming fresh air instead of the cabin's former musty aroma.

A guitar's steady rhythm drifted through the wall on my right. Grant had been playing for at least thirty minutes, the tempo switching from fast to slow and back. I stood, hands on my hips, as my ears strained to recognize the song. Nothing.

Letting out a long sigh, I returned my attention to the room. Beds, bathroom, and cobwebs were the only things between ultimate success and me. Problem was, two of those things I could handle on my own. Finding the bedding was a whole different dilemma. Grant hadn't spoken to me since breakfast. If I had any hope of getting the beds made, I would have to ask Kira or Loraine.

With the bathroom a necessary must-do, I tackled it first. As I stood on the grimy tile floor, daddy longlegs hanging around me, that decision started to seem less and less smart.

"Why are there so many spiders?!" I said, grabbing a broom.

I took down as many cobwebs as possible, then scrubbed the floors until the grimy layer had shifted into something less disgusting. Once I could safely navigate the bathroom, I tossed the mop bucket in one of the showers and took to the walls.

By the time the bathroom was functional, Grant's guitar playing had stopped. I gathered the cleaning supplies and carried them back into the main room, setting them near the entrance before heading straight for the door.

The screen slammed behind me and the wooden porch creaked as I walked to Grant's side. His door was propped open and the inside was arctic enough I could feel the breeze from outside.

"Have you frozen to death?" I said, staring at him through the screen.

Lying atop a plaid comforter, with one hand behind his head and a book in the other, he glanced at me. "You aren't that lucky," he said, before returning to his book.

I stayed rooted to the porch, shifting my weight on my feet. Grant continued reading, ignoring me completely.

"I'm not trying to be annoying," I said after a moment. "But can you tell me where I could find my bedding? I could ask Kira, but I figured I would try to make this co-counselor thing work."

"Like you made it work this morning?" he said, fidgeting with the brim of his hat.

"Grant."

He closed his book before laying it on top of a plastic organizer beside his bed. "I guess the better question is: What's in it for me if I help you?" he said. "You haven't brought much to this partnership."

"Because I don't have much to offer. Remember?" I said, watching him as he stood from his bed.

He moved slow, tennis shoes squeaking against polished wood floors. His side of the cabin was completely dirt-free. How he managed that was a mystery.

"You were off base this morning, questioning me on my ability to do this job," he said, learning against the door frame.

"You were off base yesterday," I said.

He arched a brow.

"Okay, so you weren't off base, but it was messed up for you to just outright tell me how incapable of doing this job I am. I know I'm incapable, but you didn't have to throw it out there. You could've kept it to yourself and just said it in your head or something."

"If you want things sugarcoated, you've got the wrong guy."

"So you're just a dick twenty-four seven? You never tone it down? Even when you see someone who's clearly struggling?"

"You're trying to guilt-trip me into feeling bad," he said, shaking his head. "But it won't work. You were equally feisty yesterday, and struck me as the kind of girl who could take that kind of honesty. If you can dish it, you can take it."

"Something you need to remember when people call you out, like I did this morning," I said, crossing my arms.

Grant paused, his neutral expression shifting after a minute. "You're going to make this summer difficult, aren't you?"

"Not if you don't call me out for being sensitive, then turn around and act that way," I said. "You get what you dish out. It's fair."

"That is fair, but let's get one thing straight," he said. "I never said you had nothing to offer."

"It was implied," I said, studying him.

"Maybe we were both in the wrong."

"Maybe," I said, looking at him.

He opened the screen door, and the air inside was at least ten times colder than mine. Inside, two rows of metal-framed twin-sized beds boasted navy-and-white checkered bedspreads. Besides the solitary Camp Kenton flag hanging above the counselor bed, the cabin was devoid of decoration. Once I got my beds set up, the only advantage he would have were cleaner floors and a better-organized room.

"Will you tell me where to find the bedding?" I said, looking at him again.

"I would've shown you yesterday, had you decided to work on your cabin rather than getting yourself lost," he said.

"That was yesterday," I said. "How 'bout we focus on the here and now? Where should I check? The counselor cabin or camp office?"

"Neither," he said.

"Laundry room?"

"Negative," he said. "And, before you ask, they aren't in the mess hall or any of the other buildings."

"What did y'all do, ship them off for dry cleaning?" I said, crossing my arms.

"Um, no," he said. "They were washed prior to us getting here, stored in the counselor cabin until ready for pickup, and currently lie with yours truly. I grabbed your set yesterday, when I grabbed mine. That's what responsible co-counselors do."

"Great. Fork them over," I said, holding out my hand.

"Which would take away any and all leverage I currently hold," he said, smiling. "Where's the fun in that?"

I let out a long sigh, irritation bubbling. "Look," I said. "I've had a day full of scrubbing that side of the cabin and I'm literally a handful of comforters away from being prepped for campers. Give me my sheets and quit being difficult."

"Nope," he said, shaking his head. "First you need to squeeze in the mandatory CPR training and get the other necessary credentials you were supposed to have *before* you came out here."

"Are you kidding?" I said, pinching the bridge of my nose. "We were making such great progress and now you want to swoop in and wreck it?"

"What?" he said. "You might have pulled your cabin together, but you've still got a million other things to do before you're actually ready for campers. I'm just being a realist."

"No, you're being a jerk!" I said, throwing up my hands.

"I'm not being a jerk," he said, hurrying after me. "You're being sensitive again."

"Sensitive?!" I turned on him, eyeing his smug expression with clenched fists. "I literally came here for bedding and all I got was another go-around with you. For crying out loud, you can't even have one conversation with me without being negative. I'm untrained. I get it. I'm incapable. I get it. But I'm here to stay. Get over it!"

I hurried down the steps, landing on the dirt with a thud. If he couldn't even help me with bedding, how on earth was he supposed to help me with campers?

"Why are you running?" he said, dirt crunching beneath his feet.

"Because every time I'm around you, you find a new way to annoy the hell out of me."

He slid in front of me as I passed cabin one, blocking my path.

"Get out of my way," I said, trying to dodge him.

"I feel like you're blowing this way out of proportion," he said, blocking me again.

I stopped, glaring at two burning hazel eyes as they watched me beneath the brim of his cap. He was gorgeous, despite his personality flaws, but trying to deal with someone as hotheaded and stubborn as Grant wasn't worth it. I had money on the line. He had nothing.

"You can get out of my way, or I'll get you out of my way," I said.

"Alex."

"Get. Out. Of. My. Way."

"Here we go again," he said, letting me pass.

Counselors, most of whom were more than ready for campers, sat on the counselor cabin's porch. I walked the path to the main office, glancing at Kira as Grant slowed his pace. She could be his co-counselor. She was better equipped to put up with him.

Classic country drifted through screened-in windows. I took the steps two at a time and then rapped my fist against the door rapidly. The door opened seconds later. Loraine stood on the other side, her smile dropping as I pushed my way in.

"Do you have a minute?" I said, turning on her before the door was even closed. "Better question: Do you have a replacement for the terrible co-counselor you stuck me with?"

Loraine froze in place, her glasses low on her nose.

"Because he's making me question my college fund. I'd rather drop out of school and be broke than try to spend the summer with Grant," I said.

"Sit down," she said, crossing the room.

Sandwiched by a copier, fax machine, and two rows of filing cabinets, Loraine's office had too many mountains of papers and hardly any organization; it was surprisingly chaotic given her otherwise put-together demeanor.

I plopped into one of the oversized chairs across from her desk, letting out a long exhale as I sat forward. "Let's cut to the chase, Loraine. I'm not qualified to be a counselor and you know it. Give me a job I can do, and put me out of my misery before campers get here and make everything ten times harder."

She took a seat in a rolling leather chair, staring at me. "Who said you weren't qualified?" she said, an edge in her tone.

"It's common knowledge," I said, frowning. "I'm the least capable counselor you have, and more of a hindrance than anything."

"You aren't a hindrance," she said, shaking her head. "You can relate to these kids on a level most can't. Certifications aside, you'll be a great counselor. If someone has an issue with it, they're more than welcome to take it up with me. I'm here all day, every day."

I pulled my lip between my teeth. Her confidence far exceeded my own. "You and I both know Grant would be better off paired with someone who can tolerate him. That isn't me. Give him someone else. Give *me* a break."

"This summer isn't supposed to be an easy one," she said, straightening. "It's supposed to be a learning lesson. You and

Grant just need to figure out how to work as a cohesive pair. I think you'll find you actually have more in common than either of you realize."

"We have nothing in common!" I said, scowling. "Talking to him is like talking to a wall. Talking to him makes me want to beat my head *against* a wall."

"Grant is the most qualified counselor I have," Loraine said, quirking a brow. "He's the only option for a co-counselor. Sorry, but that's reality."

"Putting up with him isn't worth that much money," I said, sighing.

Loraine eyed me behind her glasses, the look somewhere between sympathetic and annoyed. She looked too much like my mother for me to be comfortable. Another set of issues on an ever-growing list.

"I think you and Grant just need time to get to know each other," she said, sitting back in her chair. "Give it more than a few days. If you're still having issues, we'll sort it out then."

"How am I supposed to get to know him when we all he does is nitpick me?" I said. "He's hot. I appreciate that. But he's literally the most annoying human I've ever met. Are you trying to set me up for failure?"

"Not even close," she said. "Despite how you feel about him, pairing you with Grant is setting you up for success. He knows how to handle these kids, and trust me when I say you'll need a partner who can do that. If I can't get to you quick enough, he can. He's a nonnegotiable. You're paired with him or you're not here at all."

"Another ultimatum," I said, fists balling at my sides.

"I know you don't like it, but you can either figure out a way to make it work with him or you can go home," she said. "The choice is up to you."

She faced her computer. Dolly Parton's southern drawl was deafening as I stalked to the door. This catch-22 from hell left me on the crappy end of everyone's options. I could deal with Grant or leave. Stay at camp, go to boarding school, or lose my money. There was no winning situation.

I took the long way to my cabin, brushing along the tree line that ran the edge of camp. Navigating the summer with someone like Grant was like painting in the dark. There was no way to identify the colors—no way to know what picture I would get.

A gazebo sat in the space between the cabins and the pool, its wooden structure decorated with lights hung from the ceiling. In the daylight, they did little in the way of decoration. I plopped onto one of the wooden benches and stared at the cabins, mulling over my options.

That money was rightfully mine. After the year I'd had—the trauma I'd survived—letting someone like Grant get to me was like failing myself. I'd earned this. I deserved something good, out of a year full of hell.

Too much time passed before I dragged myself off the bench. I swiped sweaty hands against my shorts and headed for the cabins in the distance, resigned to my fate. If Grant was the only counselor option, we would have to make it work. This summer was more important than the issues between us.

The road leading past the cabins had counselors on either side, but I slumped up the stairs toward my side with no energy to try to be social. Tomorrow I would make that effort. Tomorrow I would try to be something other than strong-willed and stubborn.

I slowed as I reached the screen door on the girls' side, cocking my head as I surveyed the door, propped open by the metal latch at the top. Cold air flowed through to the outside, and the contents inside were way different than when I left.

Slowly, I crossed the threshold. My mouth fell open as I turned a circle, studying the beds. Lined in two rows, six twin-sized beds had buffalo-plaid comforters carefully draped over them. Beige linens showed beneath each; matching red-and-black pillows carefully rested on top.

The counselor bed had the same comforter and sheet set, but a white pillow with Camp Kenton's emblem in the center was placed neatly against the headboard. As I crossed the room, the smell of Pine-Sol was thick in the air. Even the floors wore a deep chestnut color I hadn't been able to uncover, polished to perfection and far cleaner than when I left.

As I slowed in front of the counselor bed, my eyes landed on a piece of paper lying against the pillow. I picked it up; the messy scrawl was hardly legible.

Had to prop the door open. My Pine-Sol to water mixture was too thick. You're welcome.—Grant.

My cheeks flushed as I stared back at the door, shock and awe flitting their way across my mind. If he went through all this trouble, it had to be for a reason. Either guilt got to him, or Loraine did.

Regardless, it was a step in the right direction. If he could try, so could I.

6

Optimism

An hour and a half of mentally running back and forth between Grant's motives had me lying on my newly made bed with my eyes on the ceiling and zero answers. Why had he gone through the effort of helping me? Was it fear of Loraine? Guilt? An attempt at getting my forgiveness?

I pinched the bridge of my nose and shook my head, eyes still on the ceiling. Lying here thinking about the situation was getting me nowhere. The only one with an actual answer was Grant. If he wasn't asleep.

I hauled myself off the mattress and crossed the room slowly, then hauled open the screen door to the dark. The porch creaked as I continued to the other side, hesitating as I studied his door. I stared at the door too long to be reasonable, then raised my hand and knocked quietly.

"This is stupid," I mumbled, taking a step back. "He's sleeping. He's totally passed out and here I am, waking him up, and for what? For the sake of being—"

"Completely and utterly annoying?" Grant said from behind me, making me jump.

I spun, clutching my chest as he let out a deep laugh.

"I was wondering when you would be by to say thank you," he said, crossing the porch. His shirt clung to his body; a towel was draped around his neck and the smell of chlorine was thick on him.

"I really thought you would be by *before* ten o'clock, but that's what I get for guessing." He stopped in front of me, crossing his arms. "Unless I've misjudged your reason for being here."

"I would've come sooner, but I was trying to figure out who you are and what you did with Grant," I said, shaking my head.

"It's called a peace offering," he said. "I'm good at pushing people's buttons, but worse at apologizing. I hope that was enough to get my point across."

"It was," I said, nodding.

"Good," he said, moving for his door. He pulled it open, glancing inside. "I'm going to throw this towel on the rack and put on a clean shirt. Was that all you wanted, or did you need something else?"

"No," I said, stepping backward. "I was just coming to say thank you."

"Nothing about a counselor switch?" he said, raking a hand through his hair.

"You aren't that lucky," I said, shaking my head. "You're stuck with me, zero counselor abilities and all."

"Lucky me," he said, stepping inside the cabin.

"Lucky you," I repeated.

I took another step back, walking toward my side.

"Would you be up for hanging out for a little bit?" I heard him say as I passed the metal 2 between our doors. "If Loraine is dead set on sticking you with me, I need to clue you in on what to do and what not to do around campers. We're on a limited timeline here. Unless you plan on winging it once you've got a group of moody fourteen-year-olds staring you in the face."

"Is winging it really such a bad plan?" I said, pausing.

"I mean this in the nicest way possible, but it's literally the stupidest plan I've ever heard."

He shuffled around his side of the cabin for a minute, then walked through the door while pulling a shirt over his head. I glanced at his stomach for a fraction of a second, clearing my throat as he straightened out his shirt and attemped to smooth wayward strands of brown hair.

"You can't walk into this without a solid plan," he said, continuing toward a hanging swing on his side of the porch. "That's like jumping into freezing water and hoping you don't end up with hypothermia."

"At least you'd get numb after a while," I said, following him.

"Yeah, and then your toes would fall off and you'd die," he said. He took a seat on the swing, slinging his arm around the back of it while I took a seat. In the dark, the features of his face were softer. Either he was tired, or he had lost some of the edge he'd worn earlier in the day.

I settled in beside him, relaxing against the swing while his long legs rocked it back and forth. Night had grasshoppers chirping on the path below. I listened to them for a minute, keeping my eyes more focused on the porch than on Grant.

"I think the biggest part of doing this job lies in being able to walk a very thin line between being their friend and being the authority figure," he said after a minute. "If you drift too far to one side, they see you as an equal. If you stay too far removed, they can't relate to you. It's hard to balance, even as someone who's lived both sides."

"What does that mean?"

"Don't worry about it," he said, staring at me. He rocked the swing back and forth, eyeing me quietly. "Step one is to focus on the very real campers who will be walking this porch in the very near future. Worry about them. Worry less about me."

"Fine," I said, scrunching my nose. "What's your best advice on counseling these kids? Bribery? Empathy?"

"Empathy first," he said, chuckling. "Take an interest in who they are and what they're here to get, but when all else fails bribery is a solid second choice."

"Sounds easy enough," I said.

"It is easy, as long as you're receptive," he said. "Don't judge them. Don't think you know them. Listen. Learn. Adjust. Remember, you set the temperature of your cabin. You want them to warm to you. Don't distance yourself from them."

"Except I distance myself from everyone," I said.

"Out of habit?" he said.

"Out of necessity," I answered.

I swallowed, pushing images of Nikki from my mind. Distance was the easiest form of protection. Letting people in left room to get hurt. I learned my lesson with Mitch, then Nikki. Keeping things shallow, superficial, was my best option. Always would be.

"Letting myself get attached to these kids is definitely going to be the hardest part," I said, staring at him. "If I can't, what's another option for making this work?"

"There isn't one."

"Great. Might as well pack my bags," I said, rolling my eyes.

"Take it from someone who spent the greater part of his childhood putting up walls. If I can let these kids in, so can you," he said. "You'll realize the lessons they have to teach you are way more important than protecting yourself from whatever you're trying to keep out."

"Wow. You actually sound like you know what you're talking about," I said, nudging him.

"I told you. I'm the best counselor out here," he said. "The more you listen, the more you'll learn."

"You're also incredibly humble," I said, grinning.

"The most humble of them all." After a moment, he stood, offering me his hand. "Just know things are never as hard as you think they are, but if you ever start having legit issues with your campers I'm just next door. Get me anytime."

"Who are you and what did you do with the sarcastic, intolerable version of you?" I said, taking his hand.

"There are more sides to me than that one. I just happen to like that one the best."

I straightened to full height, surveying him in the stillness of the night. Truth be told, I did too.

"Good night, Grant," I said, peeling myself out of my place in front of him.

"Good night," he said, moving toward his door.

I closed the door to my side of cabin two quietly, drinking in the hum of the window unit and the wisdom in Grant's words.

If getting attached meant surviving the summer, I guess I really didn't have a choice.

* * *

"There's always another choice," I said, glancing at the strangers filling my side of cabin two.

What was once a clean and organized side of cabin two was now an explosion of plastic tubs, multicolored blankets, and too many duffel bags to count.

Another camper pushed her way through the screen door, carrying two more duffels and another blanket. She tossed the blanket haphazardly on one of the two remaining beds, then dropped her duffels on the floor and stared at the girls beside her.

Short, with dirty-blond hair down to her lower back, perfectly contoured foundation, a trendy graphic T-shirt, and blue-jean cutoffs, she was me version 2.0. The version *before* life hit me with a sledgehammer.

Outside, the heavy metal bell clanked. Camper sign-ins were officially over, and I was already down a camper. Five fourteen-year-olds were more manageable than six. With any luck, I'd lose another two or three to sunburns and mosquito bites.

I stood, hands on my hips as I tried to muster a smile to counteract the butterflies swirling in my stomach. They couldn't smell fear, could they?

"Welcome to camp," I said, looking at them.

They answered me with collective grumbles.

"I'm your counselor, Alex. I just wanted to take a minute to let you know how happy—"

"Yeah, yeah. Where's the pool?" the blonde girl said, dragging a black-and-white swimsuit from her bag. "I need some rays. Hear me?"

"The pool is closed until tomorrow," I said, maintaining a smile. "But I'll be happy to give you the lowdown on that later. If you want."

"How 'bout you give us the info now and spare everyone the boring and basic *welcome to camp* speech," the blonde girl said, arching a brow. "Pretty sure I speak for everyone when I say the generic crap is highly overrated."

"Geez, Brie, at least give her five minutes to tell us what's up," the girl beside her said, shaking her head. This girl had shorter hair, pushed away from her scalp and pulled into a wayward pixie cut. She was makeup-less, her olive complexion accentuated by her dark hair and even darker eyes.

She tugged on the ends of her hair, leaving the strands messier. "You'll have to get over Brie's lack of social ability," she said, looking at me. "She doesn't do well with people. It has something to do with her lack of tact and basic human skills."

"I don't do well with people?!" Brie said. "Uh-uh. You're the one who landed herself on house arrest for beating up that girl."

"She was a rat," the dark-haired girl said.

"Fair enough," Brie said, shrugging.

"What did she rat you out on?" another girl said, studying the pair.

"Go ahead, Jess," Brie said. "Was it a straightener you stole? Makeup? Tampons? There've been so many things I've lost track."

"It was a watch," Jess said, flipping her off. "And it was Michael Kors so don't act like it wasn't worth the punishment."

Jess looked at me, shaking her head. "Now, if we're done discussing my rap sheet, I would like to listen to what Alex has to say about camp. Carry on, Alex. You're happy for what?"

"Y'all being here," I said, feeding into the assumption of genericness Brie called me out on. I cleared my throat, straightening beneath five pairs of eyes. "I'm so excited for everyone to get to know each other."

"You want us to get to know each other?" Brie said, grinning. "Then what? We can braid each other's hair and trade fashion secrets?"

"Quit being a jerk," Jess said, tossing a pillow at her.

Brie caught it before it hit her face, her black polished nails digging into the pillowcase. "Throw one more thing at me," she said. "One more and I'll—"

Jess threw the pillow from the bed beside her, missing Brie but hitting another girl in the process. Accident or not, the unsuspecting victim launched upright. She was hovering over Jess in 2.5 seconds, screaming.

"Come at me, Jess. Come at me."

"Girl, you know I'd rip those fake-ass extensions out your head," Jess said, getting in her face.

"Whoa. Whoa," I said, moving toward them.

"Nah," the other girl said, closing the distance. "She's had a problem with me since we got on that bus up in Gainesville. She's lucky she made the ride down here."

"You've had a problem with me longer than that," Jess said, fists at her side.

"Because you think you run everything!" the girl said. "You don't run nothing but your mouth."

"I'm 'bout to run my fists upside your head, you little—"

The girl collided with Jess hard enough to knock her into the cot. I froze for a second, the string of events playing in slo-mo as Jess bolted upright and lunged for the girl.

"No. No. No," I said, maneuvering through the oversized plastic totes between them and me.

I tripped as Brie sprinted across the room, throwing herself into the mix. Her hand found a lock of red hair at the back of the girl's head. She dragged the other girl backward, pulling her off Jess while I scrambled upright.

"Stop it!" I screamed, racing after them. They barreled into the screen door, landing in a heap on the front porch.

I sprinted through the opening, reaching Brie first. Her steel grip of painted fingernails stayed latched on to the other girl's hair as she dragged her backward. I went for Brie's fist first, peeling her fingers away.

She glanced at me over her shoulder, fire burning in her blue eyes, then hauled her other fist at my face instead.

Pain splintered its way through my jaw, blood's coppery taste soaking my mouth as I crashed into the porch swing. *Oh hell no.*

I charged Brie as she returned to the fight. Almost catching her before two strong arms wrapped around my waist and hauled me back. Cedarwood and cypress flooded my senses.

"No! Let me go!" I said, struggling in Grant's grip.

"Get them apart!" he yelled, his voice hot against my neck.

Blood soaked my chin, leaving bread crumbs on the porch as he pulled me the other way. Kira was rushing up the porch beside us, with a bulky male running up the stairs behind her. They pulled Brie out of the hustle, the guy securing her while Kira continued working on the other two. The number of counselors on the porch grew by the second, drawing more and more attention to our porch.

"I'll get this one to the nurse," Kira said, hauling Jess backward.

Jess ripped her arm away, burning holes in Kira with her eyes as she stormed across the dirt path. Scratch marks lined her face, mild compared to the bruises on the other girl. My hands shook at my sides. Grant's hold was still tight as my lip burned and copper coated my tongue.

"Erica, could you take what's left of cabin two for a bit?" he said, earning the attention of one of the girl counselors on the porch. "They can stay out here, hell they can take a tour of camp for all I care. Just don't let them out of your sight."

"Yeah," the girl said, crossing the porch.

He loosened his hold once we reached the path at the bottom of the porch. "You. Me. Talk. Now," he said.

I peeled myself away, dread curling its way through my stomach. If I turned around now, I could spare myself the inevitable lecture from Mr. Counselor of the Year. That would also make me a coward. *Decisions.*

Grant stalked all the way to the counselor cabin, unspeaking. When we reached the door, he pushed it open so hard it hit the wall behind it with a deafening crack. I followed, swiping a hand against my mouth as he faced me.

"What the hell was that?! You didn't even make it through the first day, Alex! You didn't even make it thirty minutes!"

"Um, it wasn't like I asked for WWE to show up at my cabin!" I said, adrenaline wrapping its hand around my limbs. "Everything was fine, and then it wasn't. And I'm sorry, but I'm the one who got hit. Not you!"

"Because you're totally incapable of doing this job," he said, his hands resting on either side of his hat. He let out a long breath, shrinking my ego even more. "You see, this is what I was worried about. Your lack of experience. Your lack of ability to assess a situation and defuse it."

"The last time I checked, you weren't there!" I said, frustration burning my eyes. "I was standing there, trying to introduce myself. I was doing the typical icebreaking BS I thought I was *supposed* to do. Then one of the girls threw a pillow and World War Three started. Who punches someone over a pillow?! Who does that?!"

Footsteps closed the distance between us. His stony expression was unwavering. "The kind of campers who come out here," he said, shaking his head. "The ones with a chip on their shoulder and a point to prove."

He lifted a hand, gingerly tilting my face. "And the kind who throw one hell of a left hook." His fingers raked the space on my jaw where the hit landed. I winced and he pulled them away, his lips thinning. "You're going to bruise."

"Then I'll bruise," I said, pulling away. "I've had worse."

"You'd have less, had you known how to dodge a punch."

"I know how to dodge a punch, and I also know how to throw them." I crossed my arms, watching him as he moved the other side of the cabin. "You would've seen it, had you not stopped me before I got a shot at her."

"You should be thanking me for that," he said. "Hitting a camper is a one-way ticket home."

"Then I definitely should've hit her," I said, the sarcasm in my words dying away at the reality of what that choice would've cost. Too much money. Too much disappointment from my parents.

Grant stopped in front of the refrigerator and pulled it open. "On the plus side, and trust me when I say there's barely a plus side, you were lucky enough to get your cabin's fight out of the way. Those are usually reserved for the second or third week, when everyone is really getting on each other's nerves. They'll get to see the consequence of that fight up front. Maybe it'll spare you from more."

"Or maybe they'll continue being hostile to each other and I'll be refereeing fights every day of the week," I said, moving toward him.

"That's not very optimistic."

"Yeah? Well, Jess threatened to rip the extensions out of someone's head. Hard to stay positive when you don't know if you'll be next on that threat list."

"You're a counselor and they don't want to go home. You're probably safe." He opened the pantry and grabbed a Ziploc bag, then turned and pushed the ice maker on the fridge. Ice funneled inside.

"Besides, the worst that can happen already has," he said, handing me the bag of ice. "You got hit and that girl hit you hard." He handed me the bag of ice, grinning. "I'll give it to you, though. I thought you were down for the count, but no. You got back on your feet and went after her. Didn't think you had it in you or I would've grabbed you quicker."

"I told you, I don't put up with crap from anyone," I said, setting the ice pack against my jaw.

Cold stung my skin, while contrasting heat flooded through me at the proximity to Grant. We stared at each other, silence winding its way through us. A comfortable tension slowly settling in.

"You could've called for help, instead of trying to handle it on your own," he said after a pause. "Two of us are always going to be better than one."

"And come across as more incapable than you already think I am?" I said, pressing the bag of ice to my jaw. "No way. I'll go down swinging before I ask you for help."

"That stubbornness is going to get you in trouble."

"With who? You or my campers?"

I kept the ice against my face. The tick in his jaw lay somewhere between amused and annoyed. I could say thank you and agree to ask him for help, but something about not needing him seemed to irritate him more.

"Odds are Loraine will send one of them home," he said. "My bet is on the girl who threw the first punch. She'll be the example."

"Yay! Sounds like a fantastic way to start off the summer," I said. "A camper gets kicked out and I get to go back to my cabin and pretend nothing happened. I can see the conversation now. *Ignore the physical altercation, girls. Let's move on to friendship bracelets and team bonding.*"

"Ooh, don't forget tomorrow's yoga session," Grant said. "That activity was created solely for cabin bonding."

"I hate yoga with a passion," I groaned.

Something about contorting my body in extremely uncomfortable positions seemed less than thrilling. We'd be better off with friendship bracelets.

"Then you'll have to pretend like you love it," he said. "Because the way you walk into an activity will set the mood for how your campers feel about it. Just like your attitude when you get back to your cabin will determine how your campers respond to you. It's all a response to leadership."

"Then we're royally screwed," I said, rolling my eyes.

"You aren't screwed unless you completely give up. Which I don't think you'll do. You haven't given up so far."

"I've only been here four days," I said. "Besides, I can't walk in there and pretend like everything is hunky-dory when everything has gone to hell. That's a terrible plan."

"It's the only plan you've got," he said. "You walk in there hung up on issues and they'll feel like they're on thin ice. Threatened. Like all of us are waiting on another mess-up so we can send them home."

"At this point, I'm perfectly fine with them going home. Send them all home. I'll help you co-counsel the guys, when and if you need me."

"That's the kind of attitude that's going to screw you over," he said, pointing a finger at me. "If you act like you don't want those girls around, they're going to rebel. The last thing you want is five of them against you. You'll never win."

"Four," I said. "One of them never showed, so I was down a camper already. If I lose this girl, I'll be down to four."

"Which means you'll be fighting less of an uphill battle than every other counselor here. You're on the upswing."

"No. I was hit with an upswing," I said. "See the bruise."

He stepped backward, grinning as he reached the door. "Just remember, optimism is key."

"Optimism can suck it," I said, following him.

Outside, camp was a ghost town. I scanned the trees, searching for campers and counselors as Grant and I walked the path to our cabin.

"Before you go in there, take a deep breath and remind yourself I'm on the other side of that wall," he said, walking beside me. "At the end of the day I got you. Don't feel like you can't ask for help."

I studied him, his features sharp beneath the shadow of his hat. Looking that handsome was a crime. More so when he was being temporarily charming.

"Thank you," I said, looking ahead.

"You're welcome."

7

Challenge

The rest of day one held an eerie stillness, an unspoken warning for campers and counselors alike. That warning clung to the air as day faded to night, growing anxiety and pessimism by the minute.

After dark, my girls gathered in the cabin. Despite a day's worth of *welcome to camp* activities, their focus stayed on the fight. To top it off, everyone else at camp was also talking about the fight. At dinner, a full play-by-play was the most requested menu item.

I plopped onto my bed, sighing as I tugged off my tennis shoes. "What I wouldn't do for a beer," I groaned, tossing them on the floor. I grabbed a hoodie from the foot of my bed and tugged it over my head, putting the hood up as I relaxed against the bed's metal headboard.

Across the room, the girls sat cross-legged on their beds. "Girl literally sat in there screaming her head off," Brie was saying, shaking her head as she looked at Jess.

She wore a purple bruise on the right side of her face, but the majority of the damage was on the other. Fingernail marks ran across her cheeks, red against pale skin.

"Like she really thought they were going to let her come back in here when she jumped Jess," Brie continued, grinning. "Uh, no girl. You wanted to start some beef but think you're still allowed to stay? What is that?"

I cleared my throat, sitting upright. My nerves were riding the line between mildly anxious and full-fledged panic attack. Back home, I would've fled through the upstairs window. Here, that wasn't an option.

I glanced at the girls, forcing myself to sound mellow despite being on edge. "I get that we had a kind of chaotic morning, but can we talk about something other than how Jane got suspended from camp?" I said.

"Why do we have to move on?" another camper, Steff, said. "That was, like, the best fight this camp has ever seen."

The girls, including the fourth and arguably quietest of the quartet, Jules, had spent the hours following the fight walking around like they were the unspoken heroes of cabin two. Funny, considering two of the four were involved in *starting* the fight.

Jules pushed long dark hair behind her shoulders, prominent brown eyes honed on me. "Besides, it ain't like we've got anything else to do," Jules said. "Those lame activities they got up near the mess hall don't start until tomorrow. Tonight is a free-for-all."

"Nothing about this place is a free-for-all," Brie said, sighing.

"It's still better than being back home," Jess said. "And Alex is right. I'm getting tired of hearing the replay on something we lived through. First time was fine. Now it's getting old."

"Great," I said, shooting her a thumbs-up. "So let's talk about something else. Rules. Fun stuff. Books. I don't even care. Just something totally unrelated to the fight. Okay?"

"Or we could not and say we did," Brie said, tracing designs on her pillow. "Idea: How about we switch things up and get the four-one-one on that chunk of man next door?"

"I'm in," Steff said, grinning.

"Okay. Okay," I said, waving them off. "Conversations about Grant are finished. I wouldn't want him talking about me, so we aren't talking about him. Do it when I'm not around."

"But he's a prime conversation topic, and it's not like we're doing anything else!" Brie said. "Besides, I've spent the last two summers out here trying to find any and every reason to talk to him. Now he's right next door."

"Girl, he ain't interested in you," Jess said, laughing.

"I never said he was. That don't mean I'm not interested in him," said Brie.

"We never should've changed the conversation," I said, face-palming myself.

"Just being honest," Brie said with a shrug.

I rolled my eyes and leaned against the headboard, quiet as the girls took up a conversation on camp couplings and who had dibs on who. Within the hour, exhaustion drowned their words. When I stumbled out of bed around midnight, fumbling for the bathroom, they were finally asleep.

* * *

By seven, my alarm clock had me stumbling out of bed again. I groaned and dragged myself to the floor, the thin counselor mattress leaving knots in my shoulders and neck. Moving my neck side to side, I grabbed a fresh set of clothes and my bathroom stuff, then headed for the bathroom. If I didn't shower before the girls, there was no telling how long I'd have to wait for hot water.

The floor was freezing against my feet and my body ached as I opened the first shower curtain and turned the water on full heat. I slipped inside, stripping myself of pajama shorts and an oversized Crighton T-shirt. I stood beneath the stream and letting the water wash away the events of the day before.

"New day. New me," I said, grabbing my shampoo.

The shower beside me started as I lathered my hair, but an unfamiliar singing voice quickly broke the peaceful drum of the water. Not on-key enough to be considered decent, the voice sounded like nails on a chalkboard.

I rinsed my hair turned off the water, cringing as someone on the guys' side of cabin two beat his fist against the wall. "My ears are bleeding!" he yelled in a muffled voice.

"Shut up!" Jess yelled from beside me, beating on the wall equally hard.

I grinned and changed into a fresh tank top and shorts, then threw my hair in a towel as the pair of them continued yelling at each other through the wall.

Brie was entering the bathroom when I opened the shower curtain, her hair sticking up at awkward angles and her eye makeup leaving her looking more like a raccoon than anything.

"Geez," Brie said, looking at me. "She's at it early this morning, isn't she?"

"I swear if that's Connor I'm going to wring his scrawny little neck," Jess said, poking her head out of the shower beside me.

Brie patted her on the head, nodding toward the shower I'd just left. "You done in there?" she said, looking at me. "I swear it's like I woke up dirtier this morning than when I went to bed."

"It's called being one with nature," Jess said, closing her shower curtain again.

I stepped out of the way, moving toward the sink. Their conversation continued behind me, but one glance at my reflection and my attention was squarely on the dark circles beneath my eyes.

I look like the Crypt Keeper, I thought, touching them. The sunburn on my face accentuated both the circles under my eyes and the string of freckles lying across the bridge of my nose. Even my scar was more prominent, the jagged line paler as it poked out from beneath my hair. I brushed my hair to the side, covering the scar beneath my bangs. With any luck, they would dry that direction and save me the trouble of straightening them.

"Alex, I want to check out the pool today," Brie said from behind her curtain, her voice muffled by the shower. "That means I need for you to carve out at least an hour's worth of time. I have to make sure I get my tanning in. My arms are so white they glow in the dark."

"The last time I checked, Alex owes you nothing," Jess said. "You're here as a camper. Remember? Don't get yourself kicked out. They won't let you come back next year."

"I know why I'm out here," Brie said. "But I also know I worked my ass off to pull a C average last semester. I'm enjoying what I can, while I'm here. Schedule or not."

"Hold up," Jess said, her tone dripping with annoyance. "You cheated off *me*. Don't go making it sound like you put some real energy into getting a C."

"Cheating off you was a huge effort on my part," Brie said. "You don't even realize how many times I almost got caught."

"Uh-huh. What do you want? A cookie?"

"The point is, I plan on living up every second of this free time," Brie said, poking her head out of the shower. "I wanted to swim yesterday, but we got sucked into that whole fight situation and everything went to hell. I'm making up for it today. That's a fact."

"I don't know if we'll have time," I said, grabbing my makeup bag.

"You can either make time, or I can," she said.

"I don't make the schedule," I said, digging through my makeup. "I get a piece of paper handed to me and I follow it."

"Then tell whoever makes the schedule that you want to make a change," Brie said, rolling her eyes. "Because I'm getting in that pool today, one way or the other."

"That's your choice," I said, glancing at her in the mirror. "But don't blame me when you end up with a one-way ticket home."

"You'd snitch?"

"No, but I'll chuck you under the bus if someone starts pointing fingers at me," I said. "I'm not taking the fall because you decided to do whatever you want."

She paused for a minute, her jaw jutted to the side.

"Again, your choice," I said, shrugging.

"You're right, it is my choice," she said, sticking her head back behind the curtain.

Jess exited the shower beside her, already changed into a

pair of track pants and a T-shirt. She towel-dried her hair as she walked, her voice low as she reached me.

"I get you're the counselor," she said. "And I know you have rules and expectations and whatever, but let me give you a word of advice. When it comes to Brie, it's easier to just do what she asks. Don't fight the system. Go with it and move on."

"How about no?" I said, shaking my head.

"Just trying to help," Jess said, holding up her hands. "I know my friend. She don't jack around with people. She starts the issue. Then she finishes it. That's it."

"Well, you don't know me," I said, pausing. "I'm tougher than I look, and I'll start taking orders from a fourteen-year-old the day pigs fly."

The water behind me stopped. Brie exited the shower a minute later, a towel wrapped around her and long strands of blond hair dripping against the floor. She smiled widely, staring me down like a fox hunting prey.

"I'm not like most fourteen-year-olds," she said, knocking into my shoulder, "and I'll take that as a personal challenge."

"That sounds like a threat," I said, watching her as she turned the corner.

"Take it however you want," she said.

I rubbed the spot on my shoulder, blood heating as her giggle sounded from the main room. I could handle an unruly camper, but an unruly camper with an agenda was a completely different subject.

When I exited the cabin thirty minutes later, Grant was already on the porch, leaning against the railing with a travel mug in his hand. His eyes were straight ahead and his attention on the road. In athletic shorts, a blue T-shirt, and his black baseball cap, he looked like a laid-back athlete who was contemplating life in the Texas wilderness. I could've stood there and stared at him longer, had he not turned and glanced my way.

"You're up earlier than I expected," he said, his voice raspy from sleep. "Please tell me that wasn't you singing in the shower."

"I sing better than that," I said, leaning against the rail beside him.

The smell of dew hung heavy around us, morning humidity clinging to anything and everything exposed to the outdoors. Across the road, behind the other three cabins, the sun cast colors on the clouds. It wasn't worth the early wake-up call, but it made things better.

My eyes shifted to the travel mug in Grant's hand, the smell of coffee too strong to deny. "Want to help a girl out and tell me where you got that coffee?" I said, looking at him.

"Um, no," he said, taking a sip from the cup. "Coffee is reserved for counselors who make it through day one *without* cabin fights. Sorry, but you don't qualify."

I flipped him off and he laughed.

"Perhaps I could make an exception, if you agree to take my group's mess-hall duty today," he said.

"That's not even remotely fair," I said, frowning.

"It's fair if you want coffee bad enough," Grant said.

I turned, resting my hip against the rail as I faced him. His usual Texas Tech hat left shadows on his face, but his blue T-shirt popped against his vivid hazel eyes. He turned so his chest was facing me, the smell of his body wash clinging to his skin.

"In all seriousness, congrats on surviving to day two," he said, a smile playing at his lips.

"Small victories," I said, nodding. "Even smaller, considering one of my campers has decided she's in a power position."

"Ooh, a fourteen-year-old with a chip on her shoulder. Who would've thought?" Grant said. "So, what's the issue? She jealous of your prime sleeping position, or of your ruggedly handsome co-counselor?"

"She's frustrated this isn't some on-call swim resort where she can lie out whenever she wants," I said.

"Did you tell her she could go home if she has an issue?" Grant said, fidgeting with the brim of his hat. "If she has a problem, that's the easiest solution."

"I've already had one go home," I said. "If I send any more home, my campers will start to riot."

"If they riot, they'll all be sent home," he said. "Then *you* could leave camp and everyone's problems would be solved."

"You're still trying to get rid of me, and here I thought we'd turned a corner," I said, grinning.

"I haven't made up my mind," he said with a smile.

I giggled, the laugh fading as Brie pushed through the door on our side. She stared at me for a moment, glanced at Grant, then pranced across the porch with her high ponytail slinging back and forth.

"It's the beginning of the day and she's already getting on my nerves," I groaned.

"I'm sure you annoyed people when you were fourteen," Grant said, peeling himself away from the rail.

"Nope. I was perfect," I lied.

"Doubtful." He sipped his coffee, moving for the stairs. "Perfect or not, you still need to figure out a way to work with her. You'll be better off that way. Your cabin will be better off."

"Sounds easier than it is," I said, following him across the porch.

"I never said it was easy," he said. "That doesn't mean it isn't worth it." He landed on the dirt with a thud, his tennis shoes crunching over rocks as he headed to the mess hall.

I matched his pace, mentally ping-ponging between what Grant wanted me to do and what I wanted to do. Still caught between my options at breakfast, I spent the rest of my morning in silent debate.

By the time yoga rolled around, my mind was the furthest thing from balanced. I reached the amphitheater on the outskirts of camp, rolling my shoulders as I neared the group gathered at the base of the massive stone setup. Six rows high, the outdoor space sat nestled in a clearing surrounded by trees. Grant stood among the campers at the bottom, towering over most.

"This is by far the lamest camp activity I've ever heard of," I said, closing the distance between us. "It's like Loraine googled therapy techniques and picked the five most boring options."

"Wrong," Grant said, grinning. "I'm the one who googled them."

"Of course you did," I said, slowing completely.

Hands on my hips, I scouted the area for my campers. Steff and my quietest camper, Jules, stood beside a group of Grant's guys. Brie and Jess were nowhere in sight.

"You're missing two," Grant said, following my gaze. "You think that's intentional, or do you think they forgot?"

"I think they skipped out," I said, frowning. "If I had to bet, I'm pretty sure I know exactly where they are."

"Want to track them down?" he said, crossing his arms.

"Not yet," I said, shaking my head. "I'll give them the benefit of the doubt, but if they don't show before this thing is over with there will be hell to pay. If I have to do this stupid exercise, so do they."

"Yoga is actually pretty calming. Maybe it will help get all that bubbling animosity out of you," Grant said, poking me in the side. "Channel your energy, Alex. Channel it good."

"I hate you," I said, smiling.

"No, you don't," he said, smiling too.

He took his place at one of the mats, slipping off his tennis shoes to reveal mismatched black socks. I took the mat beside him, taking off my own shoes as the yoga instructor dropped her stuff on one of the concrete steps.

"Remember to channel that energy," he said, glancing at me. "I know this seems hokey, but it can be beneficial if and when you let it."

"Is this the part where you tell me you really did suggest this camp activity?" I said, looking at him.

"My *primary* suggestion was the counselor basketball game," he said. "But yes, I may or may not have suggested this too. We used to have it when we were at camp, back in the day. I think the majority of us realized it was actually a better way to get out our aggression than what we'd been doing."

"Which was?"

"Fighting, mainly," Grant said, watching the woman at the front of the group. "It might be hard to believe, with me being so calm and friendly and everything, but I wasn't always this likable."

"You're likable?" I said, studying his profile.

He hadn't made it a secret that he was once a camper, but the occasional tidbits of information played at my curiosity. Why was he sent here? Better question: Had he screwed up worse than me?

"Occasionally, when my co-counselor is being easier to get along with," he said, looking my way.

I held his gaze for a moment, warmth filling my cheeks.

"Not that it happens often," he said.

"If you can't take me at my moodiest, you don't deserve me in awesomeness."

"I'm pretty sure that's not how the saying goes," he said.

"It's the remix," I answered.

He chuckled and held his hands out, mirroring the yoga leader. I attempted the same pose, trying and failing epically as they progressed to even the simplest positions. Despite months of physical therapy, scar tissue from the wreck kept my right side less flexible than my left. Attempting yoga was more pointless than productive.

The yoga instructor did another pose, but I stepped away—surrendering despite the rest of the group still balanced on their mats. Grant peered at me for a second, but I slid on my shoes and ignored the curious look.

"You pull something?" he said.

"I'm more agile than that," I lied, shaking my head. I straightened. "I'm just tired of waiting around for Brie and Jess. If I can be out here attempting this exercise in calmness or whatever, so can they. It's ridiculous."

"And you know where they are?" Grant said, shifting his body.

"I have a vague idea."

I adjusted my ponytail and backed away, avoiding the rest of the campers, who were trying to follow the leader despite being equally incapable of doing the poses. Steff was red-cheeked when I passed her, her breaths short huffs.

"Hey, where you going?" she said.

I continued without answering, clutching my side the minute I was out of sight. With a long shaky breath, I rubbed the long scar where metal had pierced my skin. The space beneath it was hard, numb to the touch.

"If I'm out here pretending to be a yogi, they can fake it too."

Sure Brie had her reasons for skipping, but wanting an afternoon at the pool wasn't a good excuse. The world didn't revolve around her. Neither did our schedule.

I continued through the woods, doing my best to navigate the path to camp. Luckily, daylight helped. I spotted the brick wall surrounding Camp Kenton's pool roughly ten minutes later, my side hurting worse as I continued the trek.

A diving board sounded behind the wall, the splash of water loud enough to tell me she had to be here.

"What are you doing?!" I said, stopping as soon as I spotted her lounging on a collapsible chair beside the pool.

Jess froze inside the pool, her eyes wide as she looked my way. I glanced at her shortly, fuming as I resumed my attention on Brie.

"I thought I made it clear that there wouldn't be time for swimming today," I said, crossing my arms. "That didn't mean pick and choose which activity you wanted to skip, in order to fit it in."

"Why do you care?" Brie said, opening her eyes. "*I* made time and you got to save yourself from seeing me attempt yoga. It's a win-win."

"Except Loraine made the schedule and you were supposed

to be out there, whether you wanted to or not," I said, blood heating. "You don't get to make the rules around here, Brie. I'm the counselor, remember?"

"I don't remember having a say in that," Brie said, closing her eyes again.

My fists balled at my sides, her complete disregard for anyone but herself wearing a serious hole in my nerves. "Look," I said, taking a deep breath. "You can either pry yourself off that chair and get to the amphitheater, or I can get Loraine and she can handle it instead. What do you want to do?"

"Snitches get stitches," Brie said.

"Hit me and you'll get some too," I said, shrugging.

"All right, all right. We'll go," Jess said, padding barefoot against the concrete surrounding the pool. She wrung out the bottom of her shirt, leaving a trail of water as she walked. "We both know this place, despite being a little uptight, is way more lit than life back home. Give us fifteen and we'll be there. That will give Brie enough time to finish off this tanning rotation, and it gives me the chance to get in more dive practice. Deal?"

"No," I said. "You don't get fifteen minutes. You don't even get five. You can pick up your crap, right now, and get back to the amphitheater before Steff and Jules realize you skipped on yoga to have a private pool party. Got it?"

"Don't test me," Brie said, yanking off her sunglasses. "You'll end up with a cabin full of girls whose mission will be to make your life miserable. That sound like fun, Alex?"

"Sounds like a good way for you to go home," I said.

"Take it from me when I say it's so much easier for the counselors who just get along with their cabins," Jess said, stepping between us. "We'll wrap it up now, okay?"

"I never agreed to that," Brie said, shaking her head. "I need at least seven more minutes on this side."

I threw my hands up and turned, leaving the pool before any more interaction with Brie fried my brain cells. She didn't get the point and she didn't care to listen. Unless she wanted to listen, talking to her was pointless.

I stalked back to my cabin and grabbed my sketchbook and a pencil from my suitcase. Grant could keep his yoga. This was my only way to channel animosity and frustration, without flying off the handle and creating more drama.

I plopped onto the counselor bed, the springs creaking underneath me as I settled in. Without rhyme or reason, the pencil found its way to the paper and started furiously scratching lines across it.

"Threaten me," I grumbled, drawing harder. The paper ripped beneath the force of the pencil, going through the next sheet and out the other side. "Son of a—"

"Paper say the wrong thing?" Kira said, pulling my attention toward the door.

I paused for a moment, scowling at her before tossing my notebook to the end of my bed. She was supposed to be my go-to person for positivity. Positivity would be great right about now.

"How do you handle campers who don't respect you?" I said, crossing my arms.

"That's a loaded question," she said, crossing the threshold. "And I wish I had an answer, but I don't."

I let out a long sigh as her sandals flip-flopped against the wood floor. She settled on the bed across from me, shaking her head.

"Things haven't gotten better since yesterday?"

"Unless threats have become a new kind of compliment, I'm going to go with no," I said. I rested my head against the headboard, staring at the ceiling. "Do you think I'm incapable of doing this job?"

"I don't know you well enough to decide that," Kira said.

"Neither does Grant, but he had no problem telling me that I am," I said.

Kira chuckled, drawing my attention. At least someone found the situation funny. Wish I did.

"I'm sorry," she said after a minute. "I'm not laughing at you. I'm just picturing Grant saying something like that. Once upon a time, he would've been the camper starting the fights. He's come full circle with this counselor gig."

"What was he like as a camper?" I said.

Images of a younger version of Grant spun through my mind. Him in all his sarcastic moodiness trekking the dirt paths of camp while grumbling about how incapable people are would've been amazing.

"It was a long time ago," she repeated. "It's really not my story to tell, but you should ask him about it sometime. There's a reason he's good at his job. Seeing the other side of it probably helps him relate to the campers."

"What did he do?"

"His story. Not mine," she repeated. She leaned over, grabbing my notebook from the end of my bed. "Anyway, I wasn't trying to interrupt your drawing sesh. I just wanted to check in and see how you were doing after yesterday's fight."

"I'll be fine," I said, taking the notebook as she extended it my way. "I'll just take out all my aggression on this book and hope I have a few pages left to actually draw something on."

"We have arts and crafts," Kira said.

"And put myself around campers more?" I said, quirking a brow. "Uh-uh. I'll stick to drawing in isolation. At least this way I can curse at them in peace."

"Well, I'm here if you need someone to talk to."

"Thanks, Kira," I said.

She nodded and stood, adjusting the hem of her shirt as she crossed the cabin. Once she was outside, I opened the notebook again and stared at the torn page with too many haphazard pencil marks.

If I could survive a car accident and the aftermath that followed, I could survive a handful of bratty teenagers with chips on their shoulders. I was one of them. Whether they wanted me to be or not.

Fix It

Three days and one nearly destroyed sketchbook later, channeling my frustration into drawing was doing nothing but ruining my only emotional outlet. Dr. Heichman, for all the therapy crap he'd spewed at me, hadn't equipped me to handle four teenagers caught up in themselves twenty-four seven. I could barely handle and process my own emotions, much less theirs.

Grant, on the other hand, seemed to be having zero problems with his guys. All six of them listened when spoken to, were respectful, and acknowledged his position in their cabin. He had the magic formula for cooperation, while I was hanging on to order by a thread.

"If he can relate to his campers, I can relate to mine," I said, looking out the window.

Rain dripped from the roof, clink-clanking against the windowsill. Every counselor had a night for counselor duties. It figured rain would dampen mine, drenching camp with more than three inches of water just after dinner.

The girls' junior counselor, Erica, knocked on the door just after nine-thirty. She was in charge of my cabin for the night. If she was lucky, the girls wouldn't give her too hard a time.

Erica poked her head inside the cabin, her face visible beneath the hood of her rain jacket. "I'm here if you want to head out," she said, smiling. "I'm a bit early, I know, but Louis was already headed to Grant's side. I didn't want to be the slacker JC."

"It's fine," I said, shifting on the bed. I pulled on my shoes and slipped on a gray hoodie I'd left at the end of my bed.

"Scale of one to ten, how wet is it outside?" I said, tugging it on.

"It isn't a monsoon or anything, but there are huge puddles on the road leading to the junction," Erica said, entering the cabin. She slid her shoes off beside the door, leaving mud where she was standing.

"If it helps, I think this is the worst it's supposed to get," she said, crossing the room. "We might get another storm tomorrow, but tonight is supposed to be small showers. Hopefully."

I scrunched my nose and straightened. "I'll take small showers over strong thunderstorms, but it would help if it didn't rain at all," I said, tugging my hair into a ponytail.

"Guess you'll have to stay dry," Brie said, glancing at me as I crossed the room. The smile on her face could've curdled milk.

I mentally flipped her off, then headed for the door. Grant was on the porch, zipping a rain jacket.

"It's wet," I groaned, pulling my sleeves so they covered my hands.

"It could be worse. It could be lightning," he said, handing me an umbrella.

He opened his and neared the steps, me following behind. With my luck, a random bolt of lightning would come out of nowhere, striking me down for the heck of it. That seemed to be the theme of this week. The theme of this summer, really.

Water drenched my feet the minute I stepped onto the road. Erica hadn't been playing about the puddles. They speckled the ground like impending craters of doom.

"What do we have to do?" I said, looking at Grant as he took the lead.

"We make sure there aren't campers out after curfew," he said. "First we'll check all camp boundaries. After that, we can pick and choose where to go and when."

"So, if I choose to go back to my cabin I can?" I said, looking at him.

"Doesn't work that way," he said, grinning.

Rain dripped off the end of his umbrella, hitting his track pants as he walked. Gray with black stripes, the pants showed every drop of rain that hit them. They were the worst wardrobe choice in the history of man, if you didn't count my own stupid choice to wear shorts.

Mud splashed onto my legs as I crossed the dirt, creating crusty red lines along my skin. I stopped, trying to swipe it off while Grant quietly waited.

"What on earth possessed you to wear shorts?" he said, shifting the umbrella to his other hand.

"I thought it would be warmer out here," I said, cringing. "I also thought it would keep me from having a ring of water at the bottom of my blue jeans. Nothing says uncomfortable like wet jeans."

"Nothing says uncomfortable like getting mud all over your

legs, while trying to keep yourself dry despite a rainstorm," he said, arching a brow. "You want to go back and change?"

"And prove you right? Absolutely not," I said, shaking my head. I swiped the rest of the dirt off and started walking again, my plan failing as more dirt kicked onto my legs.

"Besides, I don't think the girls want me around any more than I have to be," I said. "Not that the feeling isn't mutual. I don't want to be around them either, if I can help it."

"They're so bad you wouldn't go back to your cabin for sweats?" Grant said after a minute. "You do realize you'll be out here for the next however many hours?"

I contemplated the answer for a minute, caught between being honest and being a snitch. It would be easy to detail the day-to-day power struggle among Brie, Jess, and me, but I wouldn't. Not when he had things so easy on the guys' side.

"I'm fine in shorts," I said.

Grant chuckled, shaking his head as we passed the illuminated windows on the side of the nurse's building. "They're testing the limits, huh?" he said. "And you're struggling to get ahead."

"I don't want to talk about it," I said.

"Fine," he said, continuing to walk. "We'll spend the whole night in total silence. Sounds fun."

"Your sarcasm isn't near as good as mine," I said, rolling my eyes.

"Never said it was," he said.

Silence grew between us for a minute, the sound of rain dripping off the sides of the umbrellas and water sloshing beneath our feet the only noise around.

My thoughts drifted back to the cabin. There had to be a

way to get ahead. Four juvenile delinquents had nothing on me. Nothing.

It wasn't until we'd reached the pavilion on the outer line of camp that either of us spoke. Grant, his voice almost too quiet to hear beneath the pavilion's huge metal roof, motioned toward one of the wooden swings lining the outside of the court.

"It isn't the driest place in the world, but I'm tired of getting rained on. We can take a break until it lightens up."

"Good. I'm freezing," I said.

"And I have zero sympathy for you."

"Because you're coldhearted."

I followed him across the concrete, taking a seat on one of the damp hanging swings positioned at the corner of the pavilion. He dropped his umbrella on the concrete in front of us, letting the saturated vinyl leave its drenched silhouette beneath it.

"You're the one who opted out of going back to your cabin," he said. "I made the offer."

"I didn't feel like going round one million and two with my campers," I said, scrunching my nose. "With my luck, they'd complain some more about the wet spot in the roof. Or they'd want to know why they can't go swimming when there's a thunderstorm outside."

"Then get them in check."

"Great suggestion, Captain Obvious," I said.

He let his fingers idly drum on the swing's backing. This close, warmth poured from him strong enough to be comforting. I followed his gaze, watching rain drench the grass outside.

"Besides, I'm doing my best," I said. "I'm not the one who has the advantage of having *been* a camper. Remember? Kira said it's the reason you're so good at your job."

He shifted beside me, stretching out his long legs against the concrete. "Yeah? And what else did Kira say?"

"She didn't tell me why you were out here," I said, mirroring the movement. "She said it wasn't her story. Whatever kind of stupid excuse that is."

He glanced at me, a smile playing at his lips. "She's a good friend."

"She'd be an even better one if she would've given me the four-one-one," I said.

He let out a long breath, his hand moving to the brim of his hat. "It isn't really the four-one-one. It's common knowledge I was a camper. People who know me know the full story. You want it? Get to know me."

"I didn't ask for the full story. I just want a fraction of it," I said, rolling my eyes. "Besides, you aren't exactly an open book. Your mood changes like the weather."

"But I stay generally hot," he said.

I scowled, and he let out a sigh.

"I had a problem with authority figures who thought it was necessary to tell me what I could and couldn't do," he said, shrugging. "It caused issues back home. I got sent here to fix myself. The end."

"Who sent you here?"

"The end," he repeated.

"For someone who gave me a lecture on trying to connect with my campers, you're having a hard time connecting with me."

"I'm not obligated to connect with you," he said.

"Fine. Help me connect with them, since I'm doing such an epically bad job at it."

He raked a hand across his stubbled jaw, frowning. "I already gave all the advice I have. You have to want to make it work with them. If you distance yourself, they're going to feel it. If you judge them, they're going to feel it."

"It's hard not to judge people who are judging me."

"They're the campers," he said. "You're the one who has to make the first step. If you can't, you're setting yourself up for failure. If you can't, they win. It's that simple. Besides, you managed to get along with me and I'm twenty times more difficult to deal with."

"Got that right."

"I'm being serious."

"So am I," I said. "You're stubborn and difficult, despite this good-looking exterior. You're like a Venus flytrap. You wait, drawing people in with your charm. Then *bam!* You crush them with your sarcasm."

"No one has ever compared me to a Venus flytrap."

"Because you've never met anyone as smart as me."

He shook his head, grinning. "Where are you from, anyway? What type of background has given you this awesomeness you seem to think you have?"

"It's my Cajun coming out."

"You're from Louisiana?"

"South of Shreveport. Born and bred."

My smile faded. Shreveport was the birthplace of my parents' ultimatum. It was also Nikki's favorite city.

"And what landed you out here?" he said. "You just randomly

decide to be Loraine's niece of the year and volunteer yourself as her newest employee?"

"I'm her only niece, and I don't think *volunteer* is the right word for it," I said, watching the rain.

Grant nudged me in the side, his face tilting my way. "I gave you a fraction of my story. It's your turn to give me a fraction of yours."

"That wasn't a part of the agreement," I said, shaking my head. "Besides, it's more mysterious to keep those parts of me from you. Keeps you wanting to learn more about me. Makes it more of a chase."

"You think I'm interested in chasing after you?" he said.

"We do a pretty good job of flirting. I don't think it's totally far-fetched."

"What if I don't consider what we do flirting? What if it's just random conversations with a girl I was forced to pair up with for the summer?"

"Then it's your loss," I said.

"A-T-T-I-T-U-D-E," he said.

"I think you like it more than you let on."

"I do, but I think it's one of the biggest issues between you and your cabin," he said. "You do a good job ebbing and flow-ing when it comes to you and me. You need to figure out how to apply that tactic to your cabin."

"Getting along with you and getting along with my cabin are two different things," I said.

"Then figure it out," he said. "If you don't, that failure will fall on both of us."

He stood, grabbing his umbrella from the concrete. Rain was still cascading around the pavilion, but he didn't seem to care.

"I've got people looking to me to do this job, expecting me to do a *good* job, so I need you not to fail."

"I'm not trying to."

"Then don't."

He stepped into the downpour, glancing at me over his shoulder as he walked toward the path. I could've stayed in that pavilion with him much, much longer, but he was right. This was a job. Whether I chose it or not, being a counselor was a part of the gig and there was money on the line. Substantial money.

The rain stopped just before Grant and I got back to our cabin. I split off and headed to my side, opening the screen door to an almost pitch-black interior where snores encompassed the space in hushed hums.

Thankfully, someone left the bathroom light on. I could see well enough to navigate the path to my bed, only to find Erica passed out on top of the covers with a copy of some Nicholas Sparks book in her hand.

Quietly, I shook my head and retrieved a fresh set of clothes. After grabbing a quick shower, I changed and headed back into the room. With Erica still passed out on my bed, I found an empty one near the door and slid beneath the covers. It was lumpier than mine, the comforter thinner, but I laid there and replayed my conversation with Grant while everyone else slept quietly in the dark.

Despite being occasionally obnoxious, he was right. If I wanted to make this summer work, I had to give these campers the same thing I expected them to give me—respect.

I let out a heavy sigh and shook my head, my eyes on the window and the moonless sky. There was too much riding on this summer to roll over and let four girls dictate how things would go. This was my cabin. My leadership. My *job*.

The next morning, amid a new sunrise and too many mosquitoes, I stepped onto cabin two's porch more levelheaded and open to suggestions. Grant exited the guys' side shortly after, a travel mug in his hand and a tan the color of warmed honey. He glanced at me with eyes framed by lashes so thick they contrasted with the gold in his eyes to a point it was sinful. My lungs refused to function properly, despite my brain screaming at them to cooperate.

He slowed as he closed the distance between us. "How did you manage to be up and out here before me?" he said, a rasp to his voice.

"I thought I'd give today a real shot," I said with a shrug. "But it would be easier with a shot of caffeine."

My eyes settled on the travel mug as the smell of coffee drifted my way. "I'm craving Starbucks, but that coffee smells like a good second choice."

"You can have coffee when you prove you're trying to make things work with those campers. I need to see action in motion. Results, Alex."

"How 'bout a foot in your ass, Grant?"

He took a sip of his coffee, smiling behind the rim. "You're really a morning person, aren't you?"

He passed me, walking ahead to the mess hall. I followed, the smell of something baking amplified by undertones of maple syrup.

"Look," I said, my hand wrapping around his forearm as we passed in front of Medicine and More. "I'll admit I have an attitude problem without coffee. I'm working on it, but you're being a butthead. It's like you get a rise out of irritating me."

"I get a rise out of irritating *you*?" he said, chuckling. "No. No. You're the one who gets off on irritating me. It's a super-power of yours."

"If you weren't so damn annoying, maybe I would steer away from pushing your buttons."

"I'm annoying by nature," he said. "I can't fix it, just like you can't fix how frustratingly adorable you are when you get pissed off at me."

"You just called me adorable," I said, cocking my head.

"Did I? I don't think I did."

We reached the mess hall and he opened the door, ushering me inside. The smell of pancakes floated through the space, making my stomach grumble.

I headed across the room toward the food line, Grant behind me. After waiting a few minutes, I piled my plate full of pancakes and two slices of overcooked bacon. We reached cabin two's empty rectangular table at the same time. Grant plopped into the chair beside me, the food on his plate higher than mine.

"So what's on the agenda for today?" I said, taking a bite of food. "Group therapy or team building?"

"Mmm, we're supposed to tackle the obstacle course with our campers today. Who knows, maybe we'll get lucky and Loraine will decide neither of us is up to that challenge. Your girls will intentionally push you off the wall, and I'll be stuck trying to haul you back to camp all damaged and crying."

"I don't cry."

"Everyone cries."

"I don't. Unless I'm, like, super pissed. Then I'll cry, while screaming, while throwing things."

"See, you do cry." He took a bite and chewed slowly. "So how did last night go, after you got back?" he said. "Were the little gremlins asleep, or were they ready and waiting to go another round with you?"

"Thankfully, they were asleep," I said.

"Which means you have all day to find some common ground between y'all and sort this mess out. Tell you what. Do that and I'll make a run into Lufkin and grab you Starbucks."

"You would?"

"No," he said. "I just figured it sounded like a good bribe."

"Cruel, Grant. That was cruel."

"Sorry," he said, grinning. "I was just trying to motivate you. In hindsight, I can see where playing off your need for caffeine would make me into a huge dick. Tell you what. Why don't you ask Loraine to approve some kind of off-schedule activity for your cabin? Maybe you can win them over that way."

"Like what? Extra pool time?"

"You aren't lifeguard certified," Grant said.

"Salt in the wound, Grant."

He took another sip of his coffee and laughed. "Okay, why don't you ask her to let them have extra time in arts and crafts or something along those lines? You could go tonight, after the all-camp get-together at the amphitheater. Y'all will be out there anyway. It's not like it would be hard to get from one point to another."

"Except I've never actually been to arts and crafts," I said, trying to mentally map out where that was in relation to the amphitheater. Having missed out on a real camp tour, the only experience I had with that area was from Grant's and my camp patrol in the rain.

"If I get some time later, I'll show you," he said. "If I don't, just remember it's close to the outskirts of camp. If you reach the fence, you've gone too far."

"And you really think she'll agree?" I said, surveying him.

"She's your aunt," Grant said. "If anyone has a shot at getting her to agree, it's you."

"You don't know her like I do."

"Maybe not, but it's hard to believe she'd be as stubborn as you."

* * *

"I don't think that's a good idea," Loraine said, sitting behind her desk.

Her face was sunburned, except for the pale white circles around her eyes where sunglasses had been. Perhaps the heat was getting to her. Even Grant seemed to think the request was reasonable and he was arguably the most uptight person out here.

"How is it not a good idea?" I said, hands on my hips. "I want to try and build morale with my girls. This is the perfect opportunity to do that."

"You could also do that during one of our preapproved activities like the team-building session," Loraine said. "You don't need to tack anything else onto it. If you're doing your job correctly, those exercises should build trust between you."

"Except my girls aren't even remotely interested in scaling a ten-foot wall," I said, frowning. "They want to do something fun. Something *not* physical."

"Then they can enjoy tonight's all-camp get-together," she said. "You can't tell me s'mores and campfire songs don't scream comradery."

This was getting me nowhere.

"I want something for just *my* cabin," I said. "Group therapy, team building, those pointless yoga sessions at the amphitheater, all of those are things we do with Grant and his guys. I want time for just me and my girls. I'm trying to build a relationship with them, do this whole counselor thing the right way."

"I can respect that, but the answer is still no," Loraine said, shaking her head.

"Because you don't trust me, or because you don't want me to?" I said.

"Because I said no."

"Loraine," I said, hands on my hips. "Why are you being so difficult?"

She leaned back in her chair, arms crossed. "You want the honest answer or the sugarcoated one?" she said.

"I want the one that gets you to let me have some fun," I said. "I'm trying here. Okay? You can't expect me to do this job correctly if you won't even give an inch. You're hindering my progress for no reason."

"I have my reasons."

"Like?"

"I don't know you well enough to trust you," she said.

I paused, my blood running cold.

"I can see and appreciate that you're trying out here," she said. "But keeping you and your campers on a schedule seems to be the easiest way to manage your cabin. Besides, these activities aren't just intended for your campers. They have things to work on, just like you. That's why you're in this position. We wanted to give you a way to work on yourself, while learning how to be responsible for someone other than yourself. It's twofold."

"Whose stupid decision was that?!" I said, fists balling at my sides. "From where I stand, I'm out here for one thing and one thing only—money. I want to survive this summer. That's it. I owe nobody anything. I'm here for me. Point. Blank. Period."

"And that self-serving issue is just one of the things you still need to work on," she said, an edge in her tone.

I turned, stalking toward the door. How dare she?

The door swung open at full force and blistering afternoon heat scorched my bare arms and legs. This time of the day, my girls were scattered across camp—some at the pool and some at arts and crafts. Later on in the afternoon we'd be expected to participate in some stupid group therapy session with Camp Kenton's on-call therapist, but right now all I wanted to do was punch someone or something.

I glanced at the truck parked outside Loraine's office, my frustration getting the better of me. I headed for it in one quick movement, finding the keys tucked above the driver's-side visor. If I was so self-serving, I'd self-serve myself right on out of here. Lufkin couldn't be that far. Right?

I got in the truck and shut the door. Gravel spun out as I raced in the general direction of the exit. I had almost reached Camp Kenton's metal sign when a white golf cart crossed through the gates. Grant was driving, a curious expression on his face.

"Damn it," I said, dodging him.

The golf cart slid across the dirt behind me, speeding up as it headed my direction. I watched him in the rearview mirror. My breathing increased.

"Damn it. Damn it," I said, my heart pounding against my chest.

If I left, there would be no going back. If he told Loraine I took this truck, there'd be no going back. Either way this would end badly. Loraine was right. She couldn't trust me. I couldn't trust myself.

I slowed, putting the truck in park just in front of Camp Kenton's welcome sign. Grant jumped out of the golf cart the minute he stopped. I rolled down the window. His tennis shoes crunched across gravel as he closed the space between us.

I sat there, motionless.

"You know you shouldn't be in this truck," he said.

"You're wrong. I shouldn't be here at all."

9

Mayhem

The hum of the air conditioner in the counselor cabin broke the silence between Grant and me. I was still on edge from the incident earlier in the day, so the junior counselors had taken over afternoon therapy sessions with our campers. Grant hadn't wasted much time pulling Erica and Louis from their respective duty shifts. He hadn't involved Loraine either, something I couldn't thank him enough for.

"Here," he said, handing me a bottle of water.

"Thanks."

I took a long swig, then closed the bottle as Grant took a seat in the oversized chair across from me. He pulled his hat from his head, tossing it on the coffee table between us.

"Where were you headed?" he said after a pause. "Could be wrong, but I don't think it was somewhere approved."

"I was just going for a drive," I said. "I needed to clear my head. Hit something. Hit someone. I couldn't do that here. Not legally anyway."

Grant cleared his throat, sitting forward with his hands clasped between his knees. He was more serious than he'd been since I got here. Authoritative. Intimidating.

"Look, I get being pissed off," he said. "I get mad too, but do you realize what would've happened if someone else would've seen you in that truck? You would be gone. First flight out. I'd offer to drive you there."

"Sympathy for the win."

"I'm not sympathetic when it comes to breaking those kinds of rules. You can hurt someone, or hurt yourself, and there's no excuse. It's irresponsible."

"Well, at least you see me in the same jaded tone as everyone else," I said. "Irresponsible. Untrustworthy. Unrelatable."

He shook his head. "I'm the one who brought the truck back and lied to Loraine about checking a tire that seemed low. Despite how I may or may not feel about you as a co-counselor, I'm not lying for you again. I've got things riding on this summer, mainly the reputation I've earned. I won't lose that. Even for a girl I may or may not like."

"You only like me because you're stuck with me."

"I like you because you're real." He raked a hand through his hair, leaving it poking out in different directions. "And I'm choosing to help you get through this because I'd prefer for you to stick around. Don't make me regret it."

"I can't promise you won't," I said, studying him.

"Promise me anyway." He grabbed his hat from the table and tugged it on as he walked to the door. "You can stay here and cool off as long as you need to. I've got the cabin."

"You don't have to do everything," I said, watching him as he opened the door.

"I'm not doing everything," he said. "I'm just helping."

He closed the door behind him, shutting off the world and everyone in it. I didn't deserve him on any level, but he was here anyway. He deserved more.

I reached my cabin just after dinner, changed and ready to finish the day strong. At ten till six, Loraine made her announcement for all cabins to head to the amphitheater. I met Grant on the porch outside cabin two, feeling more human than I had all day.

"I don't even want to hear about how I skipped out on yoga," Brie said, crossing her arms as she stepped onto the porch behind me. "You skipped that boring group therapy session and for what? To go and hang out with him? I volunteer as tribute next time. 'Kay?"

I turned, staring at her as warmth flooded my cheeks.

"Hey, the last time I checked, *we're* counselors, and we have the right to decide what activities we do and don't have to attend," Grant said instead, his eyes on Brie. "So check yourself and your attitude before I check it for you. Besides, Alex is the one who went out of her way to get you an approved night out. Be appreciative. Not bratty."

"But I didn't—" I said.

"Arts and crafts, remember?" He winked at me, mischief flickering in those hazel eyes of his. Even after I'd broken the rules, he was still trying to help me out. Who was he? Where did he come from?

Grant continued down the road, holding an LED flashlight bright enough to cast shadows feet from us. I matched his pace, slowing as our campers joined the rest of the people flocking to the amphitheater.

"Loraine never approved the night out," I said, once my girls were out of earshot.

"I know."

"Then why did you tell them she did?"

"Because, regardless of what happened this afternoon, you still need a way to find some common ground with them," he said. "Just watch your back and don't get caught. Be sneakier."

"The last time I snuck out, it didn't turn out too well," I said, kicking a rock.

He walked quietly beside me; the distance between us and the amphitheater shortened by the minute. The closer we got, the stronger the bitter smell of burning wood grew. A bonfire blazed ahead, the fire crackling beneath a starry sky. I sucked in a breath, pushing away memories of that fateful night.

This wasn't home. Nikki was gone. I had to move on.

Our cabin took the steps first, sitting together near the bottom of the amphitheater. Grant and I followed, sitting behind them. I leaned against the rock's flat surface. Beside me, he did the same.

"I feel like this is some master plan to get me kicked out of here," I said, looking at him as the rest of the cabins settled in. "Like you're going to show up at arts and crafts with Loraine and get me on the first flight home."

"You don't trust people."

"Not usually, but I'm working on it," I said.

He grinned, the firelight flickering shadows across his face. "I'm not going to rat you out," he said, his face inches from mine. "But don't waste this opportunity. No truck stealing. No fights. Just you and your girls having a good night out at arts and crafts."

"Sounds almost too wholesome."

"Well, when you compare it to stealing a truck," he said. "Not that I'm judging you. I might've done the same thing back in the day. It would've been a great way to piss off my mom. Intentionally put her on edge."

"You mean I'm not the only one who intentionally pisses off my parents?" I said.

"Hardly."

"We need to trade stories."

"When the campers aren't eavesdropping," he said, flicking one of his guys on the ear. The camper turned, grinning.

"Yeah, I know you were listening," Grant told him.

I shifted against the rock, forcing myself to focus on the staff members at the bottom of the amphitheater. At some point, they pulled out stuff for s'mores. I snacked on one while campfire songs rang through the clearing. The campers below me were mellower than ever.

Loraine dismissed the cabins an hour and a half later, expecting all six groups to return to their cabins promptly. Grant stood beside me, adjusting his hat as he glanced at my group of girls.

"You making your move?" he said.

"You really think it will work?"

"Can't hurt," he said. "Just remember to take the road straight. There's a small marker to let you know you're on the right path, but if you miss it, keep following the road. If you hit the woods, you've gone too far."

"And if I'm not back by dawn, you'll come and find me?" I said, half-serious.

"Found you the first time," he said, smiling. "Why wouldn't I find you the second time?"

He stepped away, flagging down his group. Once they surrounded him, he deflected their attention while I gathered my own group. We walked slowly behind the rest of the pack, letting the space between us grow. Once everyone was out of sight, I faced my girls.

"I know we're supposed to be heading back to camp, but we're going to arts and crafts," I whispered. "If anyone sees us, head back and I'll cover it. Don't get caught."

"This isn't approved?" Brie said, a smile playing at her lips.

"No. Which is why you need to run if anyone spots us," I said, crossing my arms. "Understand?"

"Oh, we could totally get kicked out of camp for this," Jess said, her smile wider than Brie's.

"I'm the quickest person in the freshman class," Steff said. "If they want to kick me out of here, they've got to catch me first."

"That's right!" Jess said, giving her a high five.

I shushed them again, turning toward the path that was supposed to lead to arts and crafts. The trees were heavier the farther we got, but they were spaced out enough to keep them from being full-on woods. My eyes strained to see the road, the dirt often covered by overgrown grass.

"It should be about three minutes that way," I said, pointing. "Watch for snakes and spiders, or everything else that runs around here at night."

"Like coyotes and stuff," Brie said.

I ignored her and scanned the ground instead, keeping an eye out for any unexpected critters. Despite being familiar with the swamps, my relationship with snakes was rocky at best. Especially out here, where rattlers and copperheads ruled the terrain.

My heart pounded in my chest as a branch crunched behind us. I turned, my flashlight blinding Jules.

"My bad," she said, covering her eyes. "I didn't see it."

I let out an exhale and turned as the gray portable-arts-and-crafts building came into view. Marked with a large sign on its side, arts and crafts was almost identical to the camp office.

"Wait out here while I get the lights on," I said, twisting the knob.

Given that I'd never been inside the building, how long that would take was questionable.

"Right," Jess said with a nod. "We'll be patiently waiting."

"Wonder if we'll get free stuff," Brie said as I crossed the threshold.

The oily smell of paint felt like home. The memory of a paint-brush against a canvas soothing my nerves. Inside the well-air-conditioned room, the vents hummed with life. My flashlight beam ricocheted off shelves filled with art supplies, casting shadows on the walls.

"I need to come out here more," I said, crossing the room. I flipped the light switch on the other side. The ceiling's fluo-rescent bulbs crackled to life.

Footsteps crossed the tiled floors, and my girls chatted idly among themselves as they entered the room. Instead of talking to them, though, I scouted the different varieties of paints on the shelf.

"This place is amazing," I said, grabbing a bottle of Artisan oil paint.

"Not if it's one of three places you're allowed to go," Brie said behind me. "Anyway, question: Can we get some supplies for free? I want to make one of those friendship bracelets everyone else is making, but there isn't enough money on my card."

"She's a counselor," Steff said, grinning. "I don't think she's allowed to let us steal."

"I don't think it will be a big deal, as long as we don't use a ton," I said, looking at them.

"Ooh. Not totally rectangular," Jess said.

"Meaning?"

"You like to stay inside the box," Brie said. "It's cool. Some people can't help it."

I flickered my attention between them, studying each for their level of seriousness. When no one cracked a smile, I hesitated. "You call sneaking out here being inside the box?" I said, grinning. "That's like textbook rule breaker."

"You broke the rules once," Jess said, crossing her arms. "That hardly counts as being rebellious."

"You don't know me," I said, looking at her. "Believe it or not, I rarely follow the rules. Out here, I have to. That's just the way it is."

"Right. Okay," Jess said, nodding.

"Seriously." I stepped away from the paint, full attention on them. "Back home I'm constantly in trouble."

"What do you do? Skip curfew and get home around midnight?" Brie said, grinning.

"Um, no. I stole a cop car with the guy I was dating and accidentally crashed it into a lake," I said.

Silence.

My attempt at trying to relate to them teetered on the edge

of disaster. I wanted them to relate to me, but not at the expense of totally exposing my past. The cop-car incident seemed to be easier to explain than confessing my part in Nikki's death.

After a minute, Brie crossed her arms. "I call total BS."

"Call it whatever you want," I said, shrugging, "but it's the truth. Oh, plus, also, my dad is the town sheriff. Yeah. Didn't go down too well."

"OMG, that's epic," Steff said, crossing the room. A glint of amusement simmered behind her brown eyes. "Was it his car you stole?!"

"Negative," I said. "It was a random one from the station. We grabbed the first pair of keys we could find and took it before anyone realized."

"Epic," Jess said, smiling.

"Yeah," I said. "And I was epically grounded. It was one of the most boring house arrests in the history of people. Point is, I'm not this wholesome counselor you think I am. I'm just a person who's trying to make it through the summer while attempting to follow the rules. Something I think you can all appreciate, since you're walking thin ice here too."

"And you think this makes us the same?" Brie said, quirking a brow.

"I think it makes us more the same than you realize," I said, nodding. "While I can't bend the rules for y'all every day, I can try to meet you halfway on some things. But that means you have to meet me halfway too. If you can't, we'll all spend the summer miserable. I'd rather get along."

I let out a long breath, surveying the room. The girls eyed each other, their expressions neutral.

"Do you think we can do that?" I said. "Or do I need to plan on being miserable?"

"I think we can compromise," Brie said, looking at me. She extended her hand, a smile on her face. "Deal?"

"Deal," I said, shaking it.

"Great," Jess said, walking backward. She hauled an old-school boom box from the corner of the room, setting it on the table with a thud. "So, what do you say we get this party started? I've got the music."

"What is that thing?" Brie said, scrunching her nose.

"No idea," Jess said. "All I know is you turn the button and it makes the radio play. Kira had it on yesterday, when I was grabbing a new sketch pad."

She flipped a switch and country blared from the speakers. Cringing, Jess immediately flipped to the next station. It landed on some sort of pop-hits station, playing a song I recognized.

"This is good," I said, nodding. "Just make sure it isn't loud enough for anyone to hear us. They'll be doing counselor patrols later. We're on a limited time schedule."

"And she's already back to being rectangular," Brie said, grinning.

I rolled my eyes and turned my attention to the paint. Almost an hour later, I had pulled a canvas from the wall, started a rough sketch, and was mentally working out which colors to use in the background. My attention lifted for a fraction of a second, landing on the clock across the room. At 11:25, it was past time for patrols. Counselors would be by any minute.

"We need to pack it up," I said, straightening. "Just take whatever you've got and work on it when we're back at the cabin."

"I was almost done," Brie said, holding up a red-and-blue-toned bracelet.

"If we don't go now, you'll have more to worry about than whether or not you finished your bracelet," Jess said, carrying an oblong container of multicolored sand art. She unplugged the radio, leaving the room silent.

Brie glanced at her over her shoulder, her eyes narrowing. "You're such a killjoy, *Jessica*."

"Call me Jessica one more time," Jess said, glaring at her.

Steff and Jules pulled their stuff from the tables, both of them heading for the door while I returned the rest of my paint to the shelf. Once the space was clean, I flipped the lights off and met everyone outside.

We walked the path in the dark, Jess handling the flashlight while I toted my canvas through the trees.

"Do you paint back home?" she said, glancing at the picture.

"When I can," I said. I shifted my grip on the picture, swatting mosquitoes as they swarmed my arms. "I hate these things," I said, slapping my arm. "They've been on me since I got here."

"They're terrible," Jess said, laughing. "I swear they're worse at camp."

"They're worse here than in Louisiana," I said, exiting the trees.

Once we reached our cabin, the creaking of the porch beneath our feet ruined any hope of staying quiet.

"But why is it so loud?" Brie whispered.

"Because it's old?" Jess said, opening the door.

"You know, that was a rhetorical—what the hell?!" Brie said, crossing the threshold.

I picked up my pace, the shock in her voice making my pulse increase. "What's wrong?" I said.

Jess stepped out of the way, pointing at the scene inside. My heart stopped; a white wonderland of toilet paper covered every square inch of the room.

"I'm going to kill him," I said, turning the opposite direction.

I brushed past the other three girls, heading straight for Grant's door. My fists beat against the screen, louder than they should have.

Grant opened the door, grinning like the Cheshire Cat. "Welcome back," he said.

"Welcome back my ass," I said, pointing at my door. "What is that?"

"What is what?" he said.

I shook my head, trying to keep my own smile at bay. "Cut the crap, Grant. We both know you toilet papered my cabin. Own up to it and save me the trouble of dragging a confession out of you."

"What would dragging out a confession entail?"

"I swear," I said, laughing.

He leaned against the door frame, shirtless and wearing a pair of athletic pants. "I'll have you know I was hanging out with my guys most of the night," he said. "We stayed in, unlike you and your girls."

"Uh-uh. You encouraged that outing," I said, poking him in the chest. "That didn't give you permission to do your own cabin bonding in the form of toilet papering my side. Now get a broom, get a trash bag, and get yourself over there to clean up *your* mess. I'm exhausted, and I'm not sleeping on a bed covered in toilet paper."

"Your cabin, your responsibility," he said, grinning. "Besides, it's against the rules for any boys to step foot in there. I'm not going to be a bad example for these impressionable youths. One of us has to be the responsible one."

"Grant, shut up and go clean it."

"Hard pass. Thanks, though."

I crossed my arms, sighing as I glanced at my girls. "The longer we stay out here debating this, the bigger chance I have at getting caught," I said, looking at him. "Stop being stubborn and get over there."

"I'm serious," he said. "I'm not going in there after dark. That's a major risk to my position. A risk I'm not willing to take."

I pulled my lip between my teeth, trying to keep my smile from making the situation less serious than it was. "If you make me spend the rest of my night cleaning up that toilet paper, I'm going to get you back," I said. "Think long and hard about whether it's worth it."

"It's worth it," he said, shutting the door.

My mouth fell open as I glared at the screen in front of me. If Grant thought for two seconds his charming smile and occasional moments of help would spare him from payback, he had another thing coming.

10

Therapy

"Do you think they intentionally crammed it in every corner?" Steff said, leaning against a broom handle.

I paused, standing in the middle of my mattress with a handful of two-ply. "Yes," I said. "I think the whole thing was done to make our lives as difficult as possible. Don't be surprised if they also crammed it in your shoes, shampoo bottles, or any other random place they could find."

"Found snippets in my makeup kit this morning," Brie said, nodding. "Ruined the only foundation I brought out here. My face is the real victim."

"You stole that foundation from me, anyway," Jess said, scrunching her nose. "Guess karma finally rolled around."

"You never wore it," Brie said.

"Maybe I never wore it because you took it before I could," Jess said.

"Okay," I said, flickering my attention between them. "You two are supposed to be thinking up revenge plans, not arguing over foundation. We've got breakfast in approximately ten minutes. Please tell me you've thought up something by now."

"I have something in mind," Jess said, grabbing toilet paper off the ground. "But it requires some baby oil, some duct tape, and a large tarp."

"We aren't trying to kill them," Brie said, laughing.

"I'm not trying to kill them," Jess said. "I just want to harm them a little."

"With baby oil, duct tape, and a tarp?" I said, arching a brow.

"Slippery floors," Jess said.

"And how exactly does the—" The bell rang outside, drawing my attention. "Never mind," I said, setting a trash bag near the door. "Hold that thought and tell me later."

"But it's brilliant!" Jess said.

"I'm sure it is, but those boys will be heading for food and I don't want any of our plan leaving this room." I grabbed a handful of toilet paper, tossed it in a trash can beside the bed, and headed for the door. When I crossed the threshold outside, most of the cabin two guys stood on the road below.

Smiles graced their faces, amusement running rampant.

"Just wait," I said, glaring at Grant. "Payback will be worse."

"I have no idea what you're talking about," he said, watching me.

He held two travel mugs today, one his usual and the other an iridescent shade. He handed me the iridescent one. The bitter smell of coffee piqued my senses.

"Bribery will only get you so far," I said, sipping.

"This isn't a bribe, it's a peace offering," he said.

"Same thing." I sipped the steaming liquid. The hazelnut undertones burned their way through my mind—Nikki's favorite flavor.

"Either way, it isn't working," I said, shaking away the memory. "My girls are bitter. You could bring me Starbucks and it wouldn't change a thing."

"Good, because there isn't a Starbucks in a forty-mile radius," Grant said, nudging me.

I nudged him back, my eyes on the mess hall. "I was up past one, trying to get the room situated enough it was sleepable."

"See this," he said, rubbing his pointer finger and thumb together. "It's the world's smallest violin."

I hit him in the arm and he laughed.

"I could report you for violence," he said.

"Report me and you'll only be making things worse for yourself," I said.

"Ooh, I'm scared," he said, grinning.

"You should be. You just started a war."

He sipped his coffee again, eyeing me over the rim. "Right. Okay. Just remember to put your hostility aside long enough to be a decent team member in the counselor basketball game. We can't bring that drama to the team."

I choked on my coffee, warmth draining from my face. "Um, I don't play basketball," I said.

"If you're a counselor, you play," he said. "It's mandatory."

"Mandatory?!"

"Did you not read the welcome manual?"

I shot him a side-eye. "There was no welcome manual. This is some plan you've concocted in your head. Freak out Alex before nine o'clock and get a sticker. Not today, Satan."

"Except it's been on the schedule from day one," he said.

"I didn't read the schedule!"

"Personal problem," he said, laughing.

I shifted my weight, dread swirling in my stomach. "There's a spot for managers. Right? I'll be responsible for all the water bottles or something."

"You have to play," he said. "All of the counselors play. It gives the kids an opportunity to root for their cabin. Creates cabin unity or whatever bonding term Loraine wants to call it."

"My girls won't want to bond with me when they realize they got the crappy end of the stick and ended up with a counselor who literally has *zero* athletic ability," I said. I pinched the bridge of my nose. "They're going to disown me."

"If it helps, I'm playing too," Grant said. "I can make a hoop or two and compensate for your lack of skills. It'll be fine."

"Yeah. You'll get all the glory and I'll be the disappointment," I said.

"It's all about the optimism, Alex."

"No, this situation calls for a substantial dose of pessimism," I said, walking again.

He opened the door to the mess hall. The smell of bacon and eggs clung to the air. We got through the line quickly and found a place at cabin two's unusually crowded table. Our group of campers were scattered across the seats, the boys doing most of the talking while my girls threatened to prank them back.

None of it mattered. The prospective basketball game had a choke hold on my nerves. My anxiety grew by the second.

"Um, earth to Alex," Grant said, snapping his fingers in front of my face.

I blinked, fork in hand as two hazel eyes peered at me beneath the brim of a hat. "Yeah?" I said. "What? What did I miss?"

"You're really freaking out, aren't you?" he said, cocking his head.

I let out a long sigh, dropping my fork beside my uneaten food. "I'm totally freaking out," I said. "There're a lot of things I'm good at, but sports isn't on the list. I literally embarrass myself every time I try."

"You can't be that bad."

"When I started junior high, I wanted to be on the basketball team," I said, looking at him. "At our school, it was kind of the thing to do. Everyone made the team so even if I was terrible, there was a guarantee I could at least travel with them and participate somehow.

"But when I was in eighth grade, the coach asked me to help her out by being a manager. She claimed it was because I was trustworthy, but in hindsight it was because I couldn't shoot, couldn't dribble, and didn't understand how the plays we learned in practice were actually important to the game. I kind of just passed the ball to the first person I saw, which totally explains why I was always being yelled at from the sideline. When I wasn't on the bench. I think it was more of a pity move on her part. Either that, or she did it because of who my dad is."

And that was *before* the crash, when the right side of my body still operated on an equal playing field as my left.

"She *asked* you to be a manager?" Grant said, grinning.

"It's not funny!"

"Okay, okay. Not funny." He set his fork down, his voice dropping as he leaned in closer. "I can be sympathetic and serious for a moment. I feel bad for your eighth-grade self, and your lack of basketball skills."

"It feels like you're making fun of me."

"Only in my head."

"Grant!"

He laughed out loud, holding his hands up as I grabbed my fork. "As your co-counselor and someone who actually wants to win the game, I'll help you out. All right?"

"By getting me out of it?"

"By showing you a few things before you're thrown to the wolves," he said.

This close, the warmth of his skin made my heart speed. I shifted my attention to my coffee, ignoring my rapid pulse in favor of caffeine.

"Look," he said. "I'm taking Linc's duty shift tomorrow night, in exchange for him taking one of mine later on in the session. Talk to Kira and see if she'll trade you too. It will get us some time at the pavilion. I can give you an actual lesson on how to shoot."

"I need lessons on more than that," I said. "We're talking basketball 101. I need the basics, including dribbling and ball handling."

"No problem," he said, shrugging. He picked up his fork again, still eyeing me. "Just make sure you wear comfortable clothes. Once we're out there, it's basketball until you're as good as LeBron."

"That will take more than a night," I said, cringing.

"Then pack a snack."

I ate the rest of my food, contemplating the situation as campers filed in and out of the mess hall's doors. No matter how skilled Grant was or wasn't at basketball, he really was fighting a losing battle. Poor guy didn't know the disappointment ahead of him.

I pushed my way out of breakfast a little later, splitting off from him as he headed for a chore shift with his cabin. My girls would either be prepping for a mandatory hike to the lake, or slumming it up on the porch. I crossed the dirt path, spotting them on the porch as I neared.

"Definitely slumming it up," I said, turning as a pair of footsteps crunched loudly on the path behind me.

"Alex!" a woman said, her voice completely unrecognizable.

I spun, even more confused as my attention landed on a casually dressed female in tennis shoes and a faded AC/DC T-shirt. Her curly hair was pulled into a tight ponytail at the crown of her head, her eyes hidden behind large retro-style sunglasses. She tugged them off as she neared, her smile widening.

"I'm so glad I caught you! Madeline Briggs. Resident camp therapist and your morning meeting."

My face paled. Loraine wouldn't dare.

"Your aunt thought this would be a better time slot than anything this afternoon," Madeline said, drumming her fingers against a notebook. "Would you prefer to do the session outdoors or inside?"

"I'd prefer not to do it at all," I said, crossing my arms.

"Unfortunately, that's not an option for either of us," she said, still smiling. "But if you don't have a preference, I'd love to stay outside. It hasn't gotten hot yet and I'll be confined indoors for the rest of the afternoon. Does the gazebo work for you?"

"Do I have a choice?"

"Life is a series of choices," Madeline said, nodding for me to follow.

I glanced at my cabin again, shoulders slumped as I pivoted and trudged after Madeline. This was a waste of my time and would definitely be a waste of hers. She was better suited helping campers with their issues. They were the ones stuck in messy situations. I had a handle on mine. No problems here.

We reached the gazebo after a few minutes. The early morning breeze was cool as it wafted between the wooden pillars. Madeline took a seat first, clicking her pen with one hand while flipping through her notebook with the other.

"You might as well skip the note taking," I said, sighing as I crossed my arms and leaned against the gazebo's wooden backing. "I don't plan on talking much."

"You talk as much or as little as you want to," she said, jotting my name at the top of a fresh page. "I'm just here to help you work through any repressed feelings. We'll focus on analyzing the actions that led you here first. Then we'll find a suitable route moving forward so you can successfully reach your goals. Which leads me to my first question: What are your goals for this summer?"

"To survive," I said, forcing my tone to be as neutral as possible.

Madeline nodded, her pen working furiously against the paper. "And what would you define as *surviving*?"

"Putting up with my campers."

She finished writing, and her attention lifted to me. "Okay. Tell me about your campers. I already know you're the counselor for girls' cabin two, but how have things been so far? Have you found it easy or difficult to relate to the girls?"

I sat upright, sighing as I stared at the naive woman in front of me. Enough therapy sessions with Dr. Heichman had taught me one thing: They aren't interested in small talk. They want the hard-hitting issues.

"Look," I said, drumming my fingers against the bench. "I'm sure you're good at your job, and I have zero doubt that you'd like to sit here and help me with everything you just claimed to want to help me with. But I'm not a newbie when it comes to this sort of thing. You don't have to treat me with kid gloves or act like you're genuinely interested in how I'm getting along with my campers. You know what's going on. You probably know why I'm here, and you just want me to be the one to tell you so you can have me emotionally work through the trauma of my past.

"But I'm not that kind of client and you're not getting anything out of me my therapist back home didn't get. You're wasting your time, lady. Go find someone else to psychoanalyze."

"Deflection of emotion," Madeline said, jotting a note. "Have you always turned toward defensiveness, or was there an initiating event that caused you to reach for that reaction first?"

"You literally heard nothing I just said."

"I heard it," she said, shaking her head. "But you're exactly the kind of client I'm used to working with. I've been with this camp for six years, been involved with troubled youth longer than that, and if I know one thing it's that you'll turn me down on every single question except one."

"And what is that?"

"Why is it easier for you to hide from your feelings than to sit here and have a conversation with me about them?"

I paused, her bluntness catching me completely off guard. Where Dr. Heichman was more reserved, less invasive with his questions, this woman had dived straight into picking me apart.

I swallowed thickly, too many answers filling my head.

"Because self-preservation is the easiest means of coping," Madeline said.

"I'm not coping with anything."

"You are," she said, writing again. "And you can sit here for every session and try to convince yourself otherwise, but it's a lie. I know it. You know it. Why pretend it's true?"

I sank against the wood, my lips pursed as I stole a glance at the camp office. It would take all of two minutes to walk up there and curse Loraine up and down for sticking me with such a tactless person. She had to know what she was doing. This plan was premeditated.

"So, if you're okay with it, I'd like to go back to my initial inventory," Madeline said, pulling my attention away from the building. "Unless, of course, you want to continue with our current conversation."

"Ask me the stupid questions," I said, glaring at her. "But you better ask me all of them today. Next time, I'm going to tell you to f-off."

"Great. At least I'll be prepared."

Try

Friday night, despite another stupid morning session with Madeline Briggs, I happily crossed cabin two's threshold and entered the sticky night air. An evening rain shower had left the paths muddy, but my choice of track pants and tennis shoes had to be better than last time. Nothing could be that bad.

Outside the guys' side of cabin two, voices drifted through an open screen door. I waited a few minutes for Grant to exit, straining to hear his voice among the crowd.

He never showed.

Beneath the iridescent lights, the boys seemed to be playing some card game. I cleared my throat, rapping quietly against the door.

They turned, their attention on me as I watched through the screen.

"Is he still in here?" I said.

"Left about ten minutes ago," one of the boys answered.

I hung my head and did a one-eighty, heading for the steps. Madeline was obnoxious enough. Grant didn't have to add to the irritation by leaving me at the cabin, after already agreeing to walk with me to the pavillion. This was his idea in the first place. It was the least he could do.

I stepped off the porch and onto the road, walking the path while mud soaked my shoes. At night, the mess hall was dark except for a solitary fluorescent motion light at the front. As I was already creeped out by the dark, the rumbling of my stomach was the only reason I even contemplated sneaking in. Grant hadn't given me a solid timeline on how long we would be at the pavilion. If I was looking at one extended basketball practice, a good dose of chocolate-chip cookies seemed like a necessary risk.

I reached the back of the mess hall a few minutes later; that entrance was the most discreet.

I crammed the skeleton key into the lock, fighting with it for a moment before the door gave way.

Inside, the hum of the air conditioner sounded through the vents. Freshly cleaned, the kitchen smelled of lemons and Dawn dish soap.

I trekked past prep spaces, my flashlight's beam ricocheting off large metal ovens, hanging racks of pots and pans, and too many cabinets. At the back, a large floor-to-ceiling pantry sat nestled in the dark. My hand wrapped around its metal handle and pulled, the hinges creaking loudly in the vacant kitchen.

Cereal. Pasta. Bread.

I scanned the shelf carefully, rising on my tiptoes in an

attempt to spot the cookies. "Where are you?" I said, pushing a container of rice to the side.

"I'm here. Where are you?"

My heart flew to my throat as I spun, hurling the flashlight at the faceless figure behind me. Grant dodged my attack, his booming laugh almost earning him a knee in the groin.

"Damn it, Grant!" I said. "I almost peed myself."

"That's why you shouldn't be sneaking into the mess hall at night," he said, grabbing the flashlight off the ground.

I let out a staggered breath, adrenaline-spiked blood making it hard to breathe. Of course he would do something as stupid and reckless as sneaking up on me. Idiotic ideas seemed to be one of his best personality traits.

"Aren't you supposed to be headed for the pavilion?" he said.

"You told me to grab a snack."

He shone the light in my eyes, temporarily blinding me. "I was being sarcastic, but I'll give it to you. Your instincts were pretty on point. Had I hesitated one second, I'd have a black eye."

"You're lucky I didn't kick you in your balls," I said, covering my eyes. "My dad's a cop. That was the first move he taught me."

"Then it's a real good thing you went with the flashlight," he said, lowering the beam. I blinked against multicolored dots, trying to refocus my vision in the dark.

Grant ducked his head into the pantry beside me and pointed to the second shelf. "Hand me that, would you?" he said, indicating a clear piece of Tupperware with a blue lid. "If you want a decent coaching job, I'm going to need some adequate nourishment."

"If those are the cookies, you can have some after I get some for myself," I said, wrapping my hand around the container.

Grant stepped backward and leaned against the wall while I shut the pantry door. When I turned, he snatched the container before I could even open the lid.

"Give it back," I said, scowling.

"Take it back," he said, holding it high above my head.

I glared at the container, then at him. "This is not a good way to form a functioning partnership with your co-counselor."

"We've already formed a functioning relationship," he said. "And you need me for my basketball talents, among other things."

"Things like what?"

"Wit. Charm. Staggering good looks. Incomparable knowledge of camp life," he said.

"Wow. Humble."

He lowered the container and tugged open the lid. After dragging two cookies from the box, he handed it my way. "Here. I'll even share with you," he said. "You're welcome."

"I had them first," I said, snatching the box.

He shrugged and turned to lead the way outside, his tennis shoes squeaking against the tiled floors. Beside the door, a basketball and a backpack sat idly. He bent and picked both up, slinging the backpack over his shoulder as I relocked the back door.

"Were you stalking me?" I said, biting into a cookie.

"Stalking in what context?" he said.

"What do you mean what context?" I said. "Stalking. As in the behavior where you follow someone without them knowing, with some unknown reason that is both creepy and terrifying."

"Um, no. I was actually heading to the pavilion when I saw you headed this way. Thought I'd turn around and snag us a few

Gatorades. Also thought I'd help you find the path to the pavilion, since it can be tricky at night. How was I supposed to know it would turn out to be the best scare of the summer? That was just an added bonus."

"You think it's funny now," I said, shaking a cookie at him, "but I'm planning payback of epic proportions. You'll get yours."

"Can't wait," Grant said, fidgeting with the brim of his hat.

We walked the rest of the path, crossing thick patches of grass and ducking beneath low-slung branches. Ahead, the pavilion loomed against a wooded backdrop. The roof's metal apex, partially covered by a canopy of leaves, cast shadows on the concrete. Once there, Grant crossed onto the concrete first. He set his backpack on one of the wooden swings near the corner, the breeze swaying it back and forth. I set the container of cookies beside it, swallowing a last bite as Grant bounced the ball against the ground.

He dribbled, crossing the concrete in a swift move toward the hoop. The shot swooshed in the net, bouncing loud as it dropped.

"That's called making a shot," he said, grabbing the ball. "It's the primary goal of today's lesson, since goals mean points and the team with the most points wins."

He bounced the ball from hand to hand while walking toward me. In the dark, his facial features were sharper, more shadowed. He looked good. Too good to ignore.

"Before we do anything, I need to see you dribble," he said. "If you can't move with the ball, what's the point of showing you how to shoot?"

"There is no point," I said, shrugging. "I'm a lost cause."

"With me coaching you, you'll get it," he said, balancing the ball on a finger. He dropped the ball after a second, bouncing it as he closed the distance. "Pro tip number one: Remember to keep a firm grip on the ball. The closer you keep it to your body, the easier it is to control."

He reached for my hand, positioning it against the rubber. My skin heated at his touch.

"When you dribble, you want to keep your palm slightly arched," he said, curving my hand. "If you don't, you'll lose it."

He shifted my feet so they were at an angle away from each other. "If you get in kind of a high squat, it's easier to dribble with protection. Keep your other arm here."

His fingers latched onto my other arm, causing goose bumps to shoot up my skin. "Think of this as your shield," he said, moving it into a ninety-degree angle. "You can shuffle back and forth, but keep this arm here so if someone tries to swoop in and make a move you'll have a way to defend the ball."

"I don't think it will matter," I said, looking at him over my shoulder.

"We can hope for the best," he said, grinning.

He let go of me, the sudden loss of warmth disappointing.

"Now, try and move with the ball," he said, standing in front of me. "Remember what I said about defending the ball. If you don't protect it, I'll take it."

"That's encouraging," I said, bouncing the ball against the ground.

Grant got into his stance, his eyes on mine as I stepped to the right with the ball close to my side. He shuffled the same direction, shifting back as I moved to the left. He let me keep it for a minute, not even bothering to lunge for it when I lost control.

After a few more rounds, he easily stole the ball before heading to the net. When he made the basket, I frowned.

"I thought the point was to make me feel better about this," I said. "Stealing and scoring is counterproductive."

"You didn't protect the ball," he said, bouncing it. "I told you I would take it if you didn't."

"Yeah, but I didn't expect you to."

"Just because you're you doesn't mean I'm going to take it easy," he said, tossing me the ball. He got into position again, leaving a foot between us. "All right, try again. Remember to keep that arm up."

I gave him a thumbs-up, attempting to get into a basketball stance. Arm up. Feet angled. Squat. This was stupid.

"Ready?" he said.

"Yep."

I bounced the ball again, this time making sure to keep my arm up. Two minutes later, he stole it for the second time. When the ball swished in the net, I headed for a cookie.

"What are you doing?" he said, laughing.

"It's called chocolate therapy," I said, opening the container. I grabbed a cookie and ate it, watching Grant as he made a few baskets from a farther range.

"Why don't you show me how to do that?" I said, pointing toward the hoop. "I think we've established how bad my dribbling is. Let's move off it and focus on how bad my goal making is."

"First you need to learn how to dribble."

"I think we both know I'm going to need more dribbling practice than either of us can get in tonight," I said, shaking my head. "Teach me how to shoot. That looks funner."

Grant shrugged his shoulders, bouncing the ball toward the basket while I followed behind. "Fine," he said. "We'll move off it, under the agreement you'll continue to practice between now and the game."

"Deal," I said, finishing the cookie. "Now, what do I do? Any special stances?"

"It's basketball. There's a stance for everything," he said, tossing the ball against the backboard. "But the main thing is aim and momentum. If you can hit the square on the backboard, you're good."

"So, the big red square has a point and isn't just a decoration?" I said, glancing at the hoop. "That would've been helpful to know back in eighth grade."

"I've seen your dribbling. Would it really have been *that* helpful?" Grant said, dribbling the ball.

"You know, some girls would take those blunt remarks as insulting. Lucky for me, I'm thick-skinned and can dish it back."

"One of your most admirable traits," he said, tossing me the ball.

I dribbled, using my newfound knowledge. "Okay, so where on this square am I supposed to aim?" I said, pausing. "Anywhere specific?"

"Depends on the type of shot you want to make. I usually aim for one of the top corners. Unless your momentum is off, you should bank the shot."

"Top corner. Got it," I said, shooting the ball. It hit nothing but air.

Grant hurried to catch the ball before it rolled out of the

pavilion. He succeeded, edging the concrete as he caught the ball. "Okay. You have to throw it harder," he said, turning. "If you don't get it high enough, it's never going to hit the corner and it's never going in."

"Throw it harder. Got it," I said.

I bounced the ball twice and held the dribble, positioning myself closer to the basket. The shot was better than the last, hitting the rim before ricocheting in the opposite direction.

Grant jumped for it, landing on the concrete like some pro-basketball player who was leisurely shooting hoops. "You weren't playing when you said you were the worst basketball player ever," he said, bouncing it my way.

"You're such an amazing source of encouragement," I said. "Better than a Hallmark card."

"I try," he said, moving closer to the basket.

I tried to shoot again and failed for the third time.

"All right. Let's work on the stance," he said, grabbing the ball. "I didn't think it would matter, but you have zero follow-through. I can't watch it anymore. It's an insult to the game."

He dribbled the ball between his legs, holding it as he stopped in front of me. "See this," he said, pointing to a black circle in the middle of the ball. "This is where the ball gets air. It's also where you put your check."

"Check?"

He stepped around behind me, my nerves tensing as his hands found mine. Carefully, he moved the fingers on my right hand so they created a check around the little black circle. With that in place, he moved my left hand farther down the ball.

"See. It's a check," he said, his stomach flush against my

back. His hand found the bottom of my elbow and gently moved it down.

"You want this elbow to rest against your rib cage," he said, tapping my elbow with his fingers. "Keep it tucked even when you go for the shot. Your other hand provides the force, but this needs to provide the stability."

"Stability. Okay," I said, not even paying attention to what he said.

He paused, studying me. "Are you even listening to the instructions?"

"Yep," I said, grinning. "You were talking about stability."

"What else did I say?"

His face was dangerously close to mine, his body a hulking shield of warmth that left my brain deprived of oxygen and my stomach a flurry of nerves.

"Alex?" he said, his smile spreading. "What else did I say?"

"I have no idea," I said, embarrassment flaming my cheeks. "I was paying more attention to you than I was the instructions."

He paused and my cheeks grew warmer. I mean, he asked. What kind of answer had he expected me to give?

"I feel like we're getting off the topic of basketball," he said, tilting his head.

"Well, you're the one who asked," I said. "I was just giving you an answer. You're distracting. Plain and simple."

"Distracting?" he said.

"Yes. Your sense of humor could use some work, but the outside of you isn't half-bad."

"My sense of humor is amazing," he said, stepping closer. "You're the one who's too serious."

"Seriously attracted to you," I said, staring at him.

He paused for a moment, his smile faltering. Back home, hitting on a guy was easy. Knowing where they stood was easy. Grant gave nothing away. Nothing.

"I don't even know why I said it," I said, after a pause. "That was dumb."

"Hey," he said, grabbing my hand. "Hey, hold on a second."

"No. I'm good. I've obviously made this awkward, and it's pretty clear. I've embarrassed myself enough for today. We'll try again tomorrow. 'Kay?"

"You didn't embarrass yourself."

"Did you miss the part where I tried and failed at basketball, then tried and failed to hit on you? I'd call that embarrassment," I said.

"You need to quit being so sensitive," he said. He raised his hand to my cheek, his fingertips warm against my skin. "I'll give, you caught me off guard, but I think it's been apparent from the beginning that I like you. Still, feelings aside, this is a job. This thing with you and me is just an added complication. A complication I'm pretty sure neither of us needs."

Rejection stung like a knife, knotting my stomach. "Right," I said, nodding. "It's a job. I got wrapped up in this basketball lesson and completely spaced on what this actually is. We're co-counselors. I don't need to get it twisted. Point taken."

"That's not what I said," he said, frowning. "It's just . . . you're Loraine's niece and my co-counselor and—"

"You don't have to explain it," I said, holding up a hand. "You're trying to be the responsible one. I get it."

"You don't get it."

"I do get it," I said, putting distance between us. I glanced at the ball. The situation was growing worse by the second. I never should have crossed that line. *Why* did I cross that line?!

I grabbed the ball and handed it to him. "Um, here's this," I said. "I think this is the part where I leave and you stay. Thanks for the lesson."

"Alex."

I fled the pavilion, cheeks burning with embarrassment. The flashlight did little to hide it. I stopped, surveying my surroundings while mentally recapping how to get out of here.

Behind me, footsteps pounded the path. My heart dropped, the inevitable looming as Grant came into view.

"Alex," he said, still jogging. "Hang on a second."

I waved him off but he caught me anyway, his hand wrapping around my waist as he stopped in front of me.

"It's fine," I said, shaking my head. "We're co-counselors who occasionally flirt. I can respect that. I do respect that. I just feel bad for being so up-front with you. I mean, I don't feel bad about it, because it's how I feel, but I should've kept it to myself. You were just standing so close and you smelled so good, and your sense of humor sucks but it doesn't. I mean, you have a really stupid sense of humor, but I get it and appreciate it. But you just, you seemed to get me. At least I thought you did, and it was really nice. You know? I'm sorry if I crossed a line I shouldn't have. I wasn't trying to. Can we just rewind and pretend this didn't happen? Can you forget everything I just—"

Grant's hands found either side of my face, and then his lips were slanting over mine.

He was kissing me. Holy crap he was kissing me.

My nerves shot into overdrive, my heart pounding as my

hands twined through the hair at the base of his neck. The smell of his skin overpowered my senses, spinning thoughts through my head.

Beneath moonlit shadows, he pulled away first. His hands stayed on my face, warm. Comforting.

"I thought you said this was complicated," I said, looking at him.

"It is," he said. "But I never said I wouldn't try."

12

Mistakes

"I thought you agreed to try!" I said, racing down the court.

Campers crowded the pavilion benches, their cheers echoing off the rafters. Tonight's counselor basketball game was the main event, drawing every camper from every cabin. Unfortunately, we were losing. Our agreement to figure things out, despite our co-counselor status, hadn't done anything to help my basketball skills.

"I did. I *tried* to sub you out," Grant said, slowing with the ball. "Kira isn't ready to come in. Not my fault."

I rolled my eyes and took my spot beneath the basket. Kira's freshly rolled ankle had sent me out on the court with no substitutes in sight. It didn't matter that the right side of my body was crying out for relief. The court and this game were my current options.

Grant dribbled the ball, sweat rolling down his neck as he

surveyed his options. He held the ball, looking at the basket as he attempted to hit the same top corner shot he taught me about a few days before.

Erica caught the miss and carefully dribbled the ball as she sprinted the opposite way.

"I feel like I'm about to die," I said, heaving in a breath. "My body is pissed."

"We've got about two minutes left," Grant said, chuckling as he jogged beside me. "Can you make it that long?"

"That depends. Does lying on the sidelines, trying to breathe, qualify as defense?"

He increased his pace, guarding the male junior counselor who was eagerly clapping for the ball. The difference between his height and Grant's was ridiculous. Grant easily stole the ball, then did a behind-the-back dribble as he took off toward our hoop.

"Nope, not running," I said, clutching my sides.

Grant made the basket easily and gave one of the guy counselors a high five as he hurried my way. "You aren't supposed to stay here while everyone else is over there," he said, reaching half-court. "Pretty sure that's called being *offsides*."

"I don't care. All this running is going to kill me," I said.

The guy counselor from cabin one had the ball again. He dribbled, darting looks our way as he maneuvered through the players.

"Alex!" he yelled, throwing the ball straight at me.

My hand shot out with a *smack*, the rubber hitting my palm before I registered the movement. "I have the ball!" I said, panicking.

"Run!" Grant said, nudging me forward.

I did my best to remember Grant's dribbling tips, but quickly found myself tripping over the ball. Luckily, he hadn't given me more than a foot of space. He rescued the ball before it fell into the other team's hands, dribbling quickly toward the basket before the other team could take their spots.

Loraine blew her whistle as he was putting up the shot, signaling for stop of play.

"Time!" she hollered with a smile. "Game goes to the blue team."

"Holy crap, we won!" I said, throwing my hands up. It didn't matter if I had contributed or not. My sweaty blue jersey was proof.

"We won!" I repeated, spotting Grant as he carried the ball across the court.

He handed it off to Loraine, then shook the other team's hands before grabbing a bottle of water from the bench. He downed it in one gulp, his jersey clinging to his abdomen as sweat rolled down the planes of his face.

"He's so hot," Brie said behind me, clapping me on the shoulder as she came to a stop.

I nodded in agreement, peeling my eyes away despite really wanting to stare.

"Apparently he's also really good at basketball," Jess said, joining us with my other two campers in tow. "I didn't think he could game like that, but he's got some talent."

"He's obviously the reason y'all won," Brie said, nodding. Jess elbowed her in the side, earning a glare. "What? Alex is cool, but basketball is not her thing."

"Her team still won," Jess said through gritted teeth. "How about you quit critiquing and jump to the celebration part. You remember that, don't you?"

"Oh, right," Brie said, nodding. She looked at me, grinning. "The girls and I figured out the perfect way to end tonight. Hint: baby oil."

"Already got the tarp secured," Jess said, nodding.

I paused, trying to rack my brain for answers. Nothing came to mind.

"Clue me in a little bit more," I said. "What were we doing with the baby oil and the tarp?"

"Seriously injuring," Jess answered. She lowered her voice as Loraine walked by, waiting until she was out of earshot to speak again. "We never retaliated for them toilet papering our cabin, remember? Tonight is their hike to the lake. Their side of the cabin will be free."

"It has to happen tonight," Brie added. "We won't get another shot at it."

"What has to happen tonight?" Grant said, quirking an eyebrow as he stopped beside me. His hand rested on my shoulder, heating my sweaty skin.

"Game night," Jess said on the fly. "Monopoly, Uno, maybe even a round of checkers."

"Thrilling," Grant said with a nod. He raked his free hand through his hair, tugging it messily away from his scalp.

"The perfect way to wind down," I said, my insides melting at his staggering good looks.

"I mean, it isn't as cool as a fishing trip," Brie said.

"Our counselor didn't get us approved for that," Steff said.

"Um, I tried and was rejected," I said, holding up a hand. "Loraine said it's against camp policy to have any type of coed night trip. When it comes to hanging out with the boys, we're limited to all-camp activities. Not my fault."

"Forgot. Loraine is afraid of anyone sneaking off," Brie said, rolling her eyes. "Like we can't figure out a way to sneak out. Pft."

"Don't bring me into that conversation," I said, cringing. "The less I know about how and when you sneak out the better."

"Rectangular," Brie said, stepping away.

Grant's brow furrowed as he watched her leave. "I'm guessing that's the one you had the issues with?"

"Yes," I said, shaking my head. "But I've learned to accept her how she is and move on. There's no reason fighting something I can't fix."

"Wow. Is this a new version of Alex I'm just now getting to see?" Grant said, attempting to put a hand to my forehead.

I batted him away, pointing at him instead. "I blame all that running you made me do. My brain isn't getting enough oxygen. I'm not thinking clearly."

"It's basketball. You're required to run."

"You couldn't have kept it on one side of the court longer than ten seconds?"

"It's called a shot clock," he said. "If I don't shoot, there's a penalty."

"There is no clock," I said. "There isn't even a scoreboard."

"There's a clock in my head," he said. He brushed a kiss to my lips, earning *oohs* and *ahhs* as his guys passed behind us.

"Shut up," he said, waving them on. "You act like you've never seen PDA."

"Not among the counselors," Loraine said, closing the distance.

My cheeks heated as she surveyed Grant, then me, her glasses riding low on her nose. Her annoyed expression looked exactly like my mom's.

"I get that Alex is new here, but Grant knows about our counselor rules and expectations," she said, looking at us. "You're the examples. Cut it out in public. Okay?"

"Sorry," Grant said. "I wasn't thinking about—"

"It happens," she said, stopping him. "You're teenagers. You spend a lot of time together. I don't need the justification. I just need it not to happen in public, especially when your campers are around. PDA limitations are hard to enforce when the counselors won't even abide by the rules. Okay?"

"I didn't know," I said. "Promise it won't happen again."

"Thanks."

She patted me on the shoulder as she passed, leaving an awkward tension in her wake. I wasn't aware of the no PDA rule, but now that I knew about it I could make sure any kissing was done in private. Grant aside, I was still here for a reason. Intentionally breaking a rule wouldn't help me any. The last thing I needed was Loraine reporting my PDA to my parents.

Grant shifted uncomfortably, looking anywhere but at me.

"It's fine," I said, speaking first. "She didn't seem super mad."

"Yeah, yeah. I know," he said. He raked his hand through his hair again, stepping backward. "I've seen her mad and that wasn't it. Still, I don't want to give her a reason to put either of us on her radar. I've got some ties to camp. The last thing I need is one of them getting wound up that I'm out here breaking the rules."

"What ties?"

"Nothing," he said, shaking his head. "The point is, I don't want to get on Loraine's bad side. She's yelled at me before. I didn't know someone's face could get that red. It's a terrifying sight for a fourteen-year-old."

"Hold up," I said, raising a hand. "When did you start coming here? Was that your first year or—"

"I started when I was thirteen," he said, grabbing another bottle of water from the bench. "Tapped out at the max age at fifteen. Started junior counseling at sixteen." He motioned toward the path, twisting the lid as he walked.

"And?" I said after a second, realizing he wasn't continuing with the story.

"And what?" he said, taking a long swig.

"I don't know," I answered. "Why were you out here? What were you getting yelled at about? Details."

"What kind of details are you looking for?" he said, glancing at me.

"I don't know," I said. "Anything. *Everything*. Say it all."

He glanced to his right. Our campers were already headed back toward camp, the area clearing by the second. "I'll skip the details of why I was out here," he said, looking at me again, "but she was yelling at me for skinny-dipping in the lake. It's a long story involving a dare. Pretty boring in hindsight."

I laughed out loud. "Are you kidding me?!"

"No. That little scheme got me sent home before I could even explain myself," he said. "You should've seen my mom when I walked through the front door a month early. She flew me all the way back here and demanded I apologize. I guess Loraine realized how much shit I was in for if I stayed in Austin. She let me come back, under the agreement I'd settle down."

"Wow," I said, shaking my head. "I never saw that coming, Grant."

"Oh, I have my stories. Just like I know you have yours," he said, closing the bottle. "Don't think I didn't hear about that mishap you shared with your cabin. Stealing a cop car is nothing compared to skinny-dipping."

The blood seemed to drain from my body, depriving my brain of oxygen and fuel.

"What did you say?" I said.

"You. Cop car," he said, still walking. "My guys told me all about it. Don't worry. I squashed the conversation immediately. I'm just surprised I heard it from them first."

"I'm sorry," I said, freezing. "What are you talking about?"

"The conversation you had with your cabin," Grant said, stopping too. "I guess it happened the night y'all snuck out. One of the girls shared it with one of my guys. He shared it with another. It was a pretty popular conversation topic, until I figured out who they were talking about and ended it before anyone else got the details. I'm guessing that's what you used to relate to them? Good idea."

My fists clenched at my sides and all the blood rushed to my face. What I told my girls, I told them in confidence. It was meant to give us common ground, not to be spread around camp like petty gossip.

"I can't believe them!" I said, the words spilling out an octave higher than normal. "That was private. They literally had no respect for my privacy, or me wanting to tell my story on my own time. What is that?!"

"It's not a big deal," Grant said, his voice annoyingly passive. "Besides, if you didn't want them talking about it, you shouldn't have told them."

"If I'd known they planned on sharing it with everyone else,

I wouldn't have!" I let out a long breath, shaking my head. "So I guess you're expecting the whole story now, since you've gotten the secondhand account and everything?"

"Um, I never asked for the story," he said, shaking his head. "As far as I'm concerned, you stole a cop car. You made a mistake. You're human. No one out here is perfect. I'm damn sure not. Heck, I would even bet Loraine has screwed up a time or two."

"Loraine is perfect," I said, sarcasm dripping from my words.

"Okay, then she's perfect," Grant said. "Regardless, it's in the past. You've done things you aren't proud of. I've done things I'm not proud of. I guarantee you most of the campers out here have had brushes with the law. We do things. There are consequences. We learn. The end."

Guilt settled in my stomach. It wasn't that simple. Not when some of the consequences lay in a gray area that could haunt you forever.

"And I'm not out here to judge you for what you have and haven't done right," he said. "I like you for who you are now. That's it."

"You're giving me a free pass," I said, frowning.

"No, I'm not. You're just choosing to stew on things you can't change. Why? What does that get you other than frustration and more *what ifs*?"

"Now you sound like Madeline," I groaned.

He paused, his brow raised. "You're seeing Madeline?"

"Loraine thought it was necessary to cram the same kind of therapy sessions down my throat that she does with the campers," I said. "Not that it makes a difference. We've gone around and around every time we talk."

"Because you don't answer her questions?" Grant said, grinning.

"Because she's nosy and I don't *feel* like answering her questions."

He chuckled, shaking his head as he stared at me. "Sometimes you really remind me of myself. I had the exact same approach to my therapy sessions, except back in the day the camp therapist was a little more of a hard-ass than she is."

"And did you talk to them?" I said.

"Not until I had to." His attention shifted to the path. "It's a complicated story, but I'll make you a deal. You go out with me tomorrow night and I'll explain it to you then."

"Tomorrow isn't my night off."

"I'll get it worked out," he said. "Just agree to go so I don't plan everything and then get rejected."

"I like you too much to reject you."

"I was hoping you'd say that." He winked, then stepped away as he talked. "You. Me. Tomorrow. Deal?"

"Deal," I said. "And I expect the rest of that story."

"You'll get it."

13

Payback

Later that night, long after the guys had hauled too many tackle boxes from their side, my girls carried a large duffel bag of goodies over their threshold. Despite being emotionally exhausted, trying to bow out of the prank wasn't a possibility. If Loraine caught them on the guys' side of the cabin, without me around, there would be no one to take the fall.

Revenge was my idea. No way could I let them go down without me.

I entered the guys' side of cabin two, pulling my hoodie closer to my body to fend away the artic temperature inside. With some restraint, my temper had stayed calm enough to keep me from lashing out at my campers. Starting a fight would only make things worse. Another confrontation was the last thing I needed.

"You take that end of the tarp," Brie said, squatting in her all-black ensemble. She had even gone so far as to draw a pair of black lines beneath her eyes. Like the camouflage would really work. Her blond ponytail would give her away long before anything else would.

Jess grabbed the opposite end, evenly spreading the tarp across the floor. Steff and Jules taped down the sides with duct tape. When they stood, Julie got a bottle of baby oil and started slathering it onto the tarp.

"You want to help with the shower heads?" Jess said, pulling a tub of Kool-Aid from the bag.

"I'm good," I said, shaking my head.

She shrugged and carried the tub into the bathroom, followed by Steff, who hauled an entire roll of Saran Wrap in after her.

I took a seat on Grant's bed, my mind more focused on the past than the present. Parts of camp had made me better, but nothing could fix what had happened with Nikki. At the end of the day, my ghosts were ghosts. They refused to leave and I couldn't shake them.

I rested my head against the pillow, letting out a long sigh as I took in Grant's familiar scent. The smell on his blankets was fainter than on his clothes, but it was just as comforting as having him around. I took another embarrassingly long inhale, scanning his section of the room while my girls continued whatever elaborate prank they came up with.

For the most part, his space was exactly the same as mine—same bed; same comforter set, except his was navy and white; same Camp Kenton flag hung over the bed; same kind of window letting in light above our beds. The only differences between his space and mine were that his window leaked condensation and that the plastic storage unit beside his bed was semi-organized.

An alarm clock sat there. Ten thirty, four brilliant red numbers staring back at me. Beside the alarm clock, a framed portrait of five people lay flatly against the plastic storage unit. From this angle, Grant was the only recognizable one. I sat upright, reaching for it, as Brie sprinted across the room.

"Spider!" she said, still running. "Large spider."

I scrambled upright, my perception of every corner and cobweb heightened. For the most part, Grant's side was devoid of spiders. But the cobwebs in the corners held serious potential.

"Burn it down!" Steff said, running out of the bathroom behind her. "That thing is a brown recluse. Burn it all!"

She hit the baby-oiled tarp, sending the Saran Wrap straight into the air as she hit the floor with a sickening crack. Panicked, I maneuvered through the beds. She was already clutching her leg, biting down a scream.

"It's fine," I said, spotting blood before I was close enough to see the damage. I squatted, the overwhelming scent of teenage boy growing stronger the closer I got to the floor.

"Okay, so you might need stitches," I said, swallowing as I peeled my eyes away from the five-inch gash running the length between Steff's knee and ankle.

Jess reached us, paper towels in hand. "I leave for one minute, *one minute* to handle a spider, and this happens? Geez. This is why we can't have nice things," she said, handing the towels to me.

I used them to apply pressure to Steff's leg, apologizing as she gasped. "We need to get her to Medicine and More, without drawing too much attention to ourselves."

We helped her up, drops of blood hitting the floor as we tried to get her outside. We made it as far as the porch before she stopped, shaking her head with a frown.

"There's no way I can walk there," she said, tears streaming down her cheeks. "I have this fear of blood and I feel like I'm literally about to pass out. I'm trying but I can't. I just can't."

I looked at Jess and Jules. "Okay. Can y'all go get the nurse? Tell her one of our campers fell walking into the bathroom and we're having a hard time getting her to the nurse's station. There's a golf cart she can use."

"I thought someone stole the golf cart?" Jess said.

"They found it behind the mess hall," Brie said, shaking her head. "Remember? It went missing from the office but someone found it at the mess hall. Loraine was talking about it the other day."

"Just get to the nurse's office," I said, looking at Jess again. "The quicker she gets here, the more time I have to get the guys' side back in order. The last thing anyone needs is Grant or one of his campers breaking themselves."

"I mean, that was the goal," Brie said.

"For crying out loud!" I said, looking at her.

Jess and Jules fled the porch while I kept a wary eye on Brie. Her lack of sympathy for anyone and anything was astounding, to say the least.

"Do you think you can manage to stay out here until the nurse shows up?" I said in a breath. "I'm going to start working on that tarp."

"You're really going to kill our prank?" Brie said, crossing her arms.

"It's better than hurting someone," I said, standing.

I didn't wait for her response before racing across the porch.

If the nurse rolled up quicker than I planned, it would be hard explaining why I was on the guys' side. It would be even harder if being in there after dark was really as serious as Grant had made it seem.

Inside the room, Steff's blood left a trail from the door to the spot where she had landed on the floor. I avoided the blood and squatted beside the tarp, cringing as baby oil coated my fingers.

"This was stupid," I said, rolling the tarp as quickly as I could. "Why did I agree to this?"

Shuffling to the left, I continued folding the tarp like a burrito. By the time I was comfortable with the baby-oiled blob, the crunching of gravel beneath a golf cart yanked me outside.

Night air hit me as my feet touched the porch. Nurse Harriet was already hopping off her golf cart. Luckily, her interest was focused on Steff and far away from me.

"Can you move it?" she said, her frizzy black curls blowing in the breeze.

"Yeah, but it hurts," Steff said, looking at her.

I discreetly crossed the porch, avoiding the nurse's line of sight. "I think it's superficial," she said, checking the leg. "But we need to get it cleaned and bandaged. Y'all help me get her on the cart."

I moved from my position close to Grant's door, hooking Steff's arm around my shoulder as the other girls helped her stand. Two minutes later, she was loaded on the cart, gagging over the sight of blood on her shoes.

"But it's *her* blood," Brie said as they drove off. "If anyone should be gagging, it should be us."

"You're heartless," Jess said, shaking her head.

"Am I wrong?"

"It doesn't matter," I interrupted, drawing their attention.

I stood in the middle of the porch, filthy and too exhausted to function. An argument over the legitimacy of Steff's blood phobia was the last thing I wanted to hear. My brain couldn't take the conflict. *I* couldn't take the conflict.

"I think the three of you should head to bed," I said, shifting my weight. "Grant's guys will be back any minute. I'm going to finish the cleanup in his cabin before they get here. If they have any questions, I would rather be the one to answer them."

"You weren't the only one who made the mess," Jess said, stepping forward. "We can help."

"I got this," I said, holding up a hand. "You three go to bed."

Her lips spread into a thin line, the look on her face shifting into something I hadn't seen in a while. Maybe my tone was the reason, maybe something else, but Jess gave a huff and turned for our side of the cabin.

"We didn't mean for someone to actually get hurt," Jules said, lingering outside as Brie and Jess exited through the door. "It was an accident. Please don't be mad."

"I never said I was mad," I said. "I'm just doing my duty as a counselor and ensuring no one else gets hurt. That means the three of you need to be in there while I handle the guy's side. Easy."

"And that's the only issue?" she said, crossing her arms.

"That's the only issue," I said, turning my back on her.

I walked into Grant's side of the cabin, letting out a long sigh. I had to get his side pulled together before I crashed completely. With the way the night was going, that task was getting harder by the minute.

I grabbed the tarp, heaving it across the porch to our side of the cabin with a trail of baby oil dripping behind me. It was easier to rinse it in our shower. Then I could dry it quickly and store it in one of the closets before questions were asked.

"Sure you don't want us to help?" Jess said, changing clothes as I dropped the tarp in a shower.

I shook my head and moved back toward the door, returning to Grant's side a few seconds later. Except for the blood, the room looked almost normal. Good. At least I was on the right track.

I hurried to the bathroom and grabbed a handful of paper towels and some cleaning supplies from beneath the sink. Short on time, non-watered-down Pine Sol would have to do the job.

With my nerves on edge and my heart in my throat, I quickly scrubbed what blood spots I could find on the floor. After finishing, I carried the bottle back to the bathroom and tossed the paper towels in the trash. Buried beneath a mountain of clean ones, nobody would notice them there. Hopefully.

Maneuvering through the guys' side one last time, I switched off the light in the bathroom and returned to Grant's bed, fixing the blankets I'd ruffled. My eyes briefly landed on the picture beside his bed. Three kids, two adults, and a dog looked back at me, all of them standing in front of the Camp Kenton sign still present today.

With the youngest kid in the picture looking strikingly like Grant, there was no denying this was his family. I grabbed the picture carefully, scanning it with close attention.

Dark hair ran in his family; all five boasted chestnut-colored locks. His mom had her hands on either side of his shoulders and was wearing a power suit instead of street clothes like everyone else. She looked important, the kind of woman who could walk into a room and demand attention. Just like Grant.

I studied her a little longer, feeling a pang of familiarity. I hadn't met her, but I recognized her from somewhere. *Where?*

Footsteps on the porch drew my attention and my pulse raced again. If Loraine caught wind of the accident, and found me here, it was game over.

I turned, sneaking across the wood floor until I spotted Jess creeping across the threshold. I let out a long breath, my hand at the base of my throat.

"I thought you were Loraine," I whispered.

"Not even close," she said. "But I saw the guys through our back window and they're almost to cabin four. Unless you intend to get caught, you need to hurry."

"I'm done," I said, racing toward the door.

We closed the screen door to our side just before Grant and his boys reached the porch. They spoke in hushed tones, contradicting their heavy footsteps.

"Could they be any louder?" Brie groaned, tugging up her covers.

"Let them enjoy tonight," Jess said, sitting on the bed beside her. "They'll be much quieter in the morning. Just wait."

14

Complicated

"Hi, best co-counselor ever," Grant said, catching me outside at the normal time.

He was leaning against the porch railing like every other day, holding two travel mugs with extra cream in mine.

"You wouldn't happen to know why some of my campers are currently blue, would you?"

I paused, mentally face-palming myself. "I want it noted that I cleaned up the most dangerous part," I said continuing toward him.

"Heard one of your girls spent last night in the nurse's office," he said, handing me my coffee. "All things considered, I'd take blue humans over broken ones."

Despite the guilt still nagging my conscience, Grant's smile was contagious. Seeing him at the beginning of every day was comforting, a ritual that made the day seem more manageable.

"On a scale of one to ten, how Smurfish are they?" I said.

"Mm, a solid nine, but the Saran-Wrapped toilet seats were the real winner. That was a pain, considering most of them take a morning crap."

Of course they wrapped the toilet seats. Brie was in charge.

"Loraine is totally going to catch wind of it and realize my cabin is the one responsible," I said, cringing.

"I'll just lie and say it was an innocent prank between my campers," Grant said. "She trusts me. There's no reason to suspect I'm lying."

"Unless it's to cover for me. She knows we like each other. It would make sense for you to lie for me."

"Then I'll take one for the team and make sure there's a five-foot radius between us today," he said, backing away. "She'll think we're arguing about something, and we'll fly under the radar. Besides, I know how hard it is for you to keep your hands off me. The five-foot radius will help you control those urges."

"Hey! Most of the time *you* start it."

"Can you blame a guy?"

Grant closed the distance, a smile playing at his lips. Whether or not he was always the one to initiate affection, I had zero problem following through. Being around him was natural. Too natural for someone trying to stick to the rules.

"Kissing you is totally worth the lecture," he said.

"You're being a bad influence."

"I never claimed to be a good one."

He grabbed my hand, linking it with his.

"In other camp matters, what do you want to do about this prank war?" he said. "I like knowing you tried and failed to get revenge, but I don't like knowing you were almost caught. Loraine won't take it easy on you just because you're her niece."

"That's the best reason *to* take it easy on me."

"Except she has to file a report every time one of the campers gets hurt," Grant said. "Then that report is sent to other people, then forwarded to more people. Eventually, a board who puts it with the rest of Camp Kenton's documentation reviews it. It can be a big deal if the wrong person gets injured, or if anyone gets injured too bad."

"You seem to know a lot about the inner workings of camp," I said.

"Probably because I have connections to the people in charge of running said camp."

I surveyed him as he walked toward the porch steps. "What connections?"

"None-ya business," he said, taking them one-by-one. "So, not to change the topic, but are you and me still on for tonight? Or have you come up with some lame excuse for why you can't and won't go on a date with me?"

"Answer my question, then I'll answer yours."

"But talking about a potential date is funner than talking about camp. We live and breathe this every day. Don't drag my boring outside life into the mix."

"So it has to do with your outside life?" I said, quirking a brow.

"It has to do with my mom," he said, landing on the dirt. "And that's all the information you're getting. You want more, you can get it on the date."

"Um, you turned me down first," I said, heading for the steps. "If I recall correctly, which I do ninety percent of the time, I hit on you and you rejected me. It would serve you right for me to dish some of that disappointment your direction."

"You wouldn't turn down Starbucks."

"Starbucks? Who said Starbucks? That should've been your starting point," I said.

He nudged me in my side, then grabbed my hand as we walked. "Just be at the counselor cabin by nine."

"You drive a hard bargain, Grant."

"It's the *only* bargain, Alex."

* * *

A quarter after eight, Kira poked her head through cabin two's screen door. I pushed myself off my bed, sliding on a pair of sandals as she headed my way.

"Um, excuse me, but where do you think you're headed with your hair all curled and your makeup looking like a YouTube tutorial done right?" Brie said, not even bothering to lift her head off her pillow. "And don't bother telling me it isn't somewhere exciting. You haven't contoured since you got here. Trust me, I've been dying to help you."

"I feel like that's her way of complimenting you," Kira said, meeting me in the middle of the cabin.

"It's the closest she'll get," Jess said.

I grinned and shook my head, fumbling with the earrings Kira had lent me. I'd been around Grant for a while now, but mid-hair-curling my stomach had started to knot.

It was stupid. He liked me. I liked him. Still, doing something relatively normal with a guy I was legit interested in was oddly uncomfortable. What if outside of camp, we didn't have the same kind of chemistry? I mean, here we had to be around each other. Outside camp, we didn't *have* to do anything.

"Hey," Kira said, tilting her face into view.

I shook the thoughts, absentmindedly smoothing the front of my romper.

"You have a great time and make sure you give me all the deets later," she said. "I'll be here holding down the fort when you get back."

"Thanks, Kira," I said, nodding.

I tucked a piece of hair behind my ear and let out a long breath, slowly closing the distance between me and the door.

Outside, amid the quiet, most of the cabins were shut down for the night. Lights were off, the hum of the grasshoppers the only noise to disturb the silence. Dirt crunched beneath my feet, the distance between cabin two and the counselor cabin shrinking as my heart started to race.

Why would I get nervous now? When Grant and I were on great terms? *Because every time you let someone in, you lose them.*

Guilt simmered in my stomach, boiling harder as I found my way to the counselor cabin's porch. That wasn't true. *It is true.*

My arms wrapped around my stomach, any excitement for the date dying a slow and miserable death as my mind drifted further into memories of Mitch. Memories of Nikki.

"Quit thinking about it," I whispered, skirting a glance around camp.

Grant would be here any minute, and I would have to find a way to force a smile before he realized something was wrong. I could hide my emotions from literally every human on earth, but I couldn't do it if I didn't have time to collect myself. I couldn't do it if—

"Hey, beautiful."

The words ignited heat in my veins, pulling my attention toward the faceless silhouette stalking toward me in the dark. Grant's face became more visible the closer he came. His smile was brighter than before. Warm.

He was dressed in a plaid button-down shirt and khaki cargo shorts, his head devoid of his usual Texas Tech hat, leaving his overgrown hair poking out behind his ears. And he smelled good. Real good. Like vanilla and sandalwood and every other delicious aroma I couldn't even think of at the moment.

With his hazel eyes on full display and a five-o'clock shadow gracing his chin, the planes of his face sucked every coherent thought from my brain. It wasn't fair to look this good, not when I was trying to wage a war between why I should and shouldn't let him in.

"You ready?" he said, twirling a pair of car keys in his hand.

"That depends. Are those the keys to Loraine's truck?"

"Why? You want them to be?" he said. He flashed me another grin when I shook my head. "They're the keys to Linc's car. I'm borrowing it in exchange for covering his lifeguard shift for the next four days."

"And what about *your* shift out at arts and crafts?" I said, quirking a brow. "Because I happen to know a particular co-counselor of yours who was assigned to cover the pavilion for the next few days, but would be more than happy to bribe a junior counselor into doing it for her."

"Ah, I don't know. Loraine has this thing about people switching shifts—"

I nudged him in the side and he laughed.

"Okay. Okay. You get Erica to cover your shift at the pavilion and I'll happily have you fill in for me at A and C. We both know that's where you want to be anyway."

"Air-conditioning. Unlimited painting supplies. No arguments over who kicked a ball out of bounds or who fouled who. You can't blame me."

"I don't know. Maybe it would give you some time to work on your basketball skills," Grant said.

He grabbed my hand, linking his fingers with mine as we stepped off the porch. We were barely past the camp office when he stopped again, his body a wall of warmth as he turned and faced me.

"Hi, I'm Alex," I said, grinning as I looked at him. "Who are you? How can I get your number?"

"Shh," he said, putting a finger to my lips. "Your aunt is outside her RV and I'm trying real hard not to get us caught."

"Why does it matter?" I said, peering around him. "Our shifts are covered."

"They are," he whispered, "but that doesn't give us permission to leave camp. Nights off are usually spent in the counselor cabin, down at the lake, or somewhere near camp. If she realizes we don't plan on staying here, she'll flip."

My pulse raced at the sight of Loraine. She was sipping from a cup, sitting quietly beneath her awning, while a TV sounded through the camper's screen door. She was like the security guard outside the party, waiting to catch stragglers.

"Any ideas for how to get by her?" I said, looking at him again.

"Well, we could wait it out or we could take the other way through camp. That would involve the woods and possibly getting snake-bit, but I'm up for it if you are."

"Danger on the first date?" I said. "Somebody knows the way to my heart."

Grant shifted, holding my hand tighter as he turned and headed the opposite direction. In the dark of night, Camp Kenton was a ghost town. The trees lining it even more so, their overbearing stature and impending darkness making my heart race as he entered them with me following behind.

"Why do I feel like we're going the complete wrong direction?"

"Because your sense of direction sucks," he said, laughing.

I squeezed his hand tighter but he continued walking, holding back low-slung tree limbs and dodging broken branches as we weaved a darkening path through the woods.

"This looks straight out of a horror movie," I said. "Like something is about to swoop in and grab us."

"We're almost there," he said. "But in the event this turns into *The Blair Witch Project*, I'm sacrificing you."

"Aw thanks. That makes me feel all warm and cozy inside."

Ahead, through a series of narrowing trees, the faint outline of a parking lot slowly started to appear. Grant continued toward it, maintaining his grip on my hand as the cars became more and more clear.

"Oh, ye of little faith," he said as we exited the last of the trees, crossing the dirt toward the moonlit parking lot.

"Let me check myself for ticks. Then we'll discuss how much faith I have in you," I said, smiling as he stopped beside a black four-door SUV.

"I can help you check for ticks."

"You wish."

"I do."

I grinned and slid into the passenger side. He closed the door behind me, hurrying around the hood to the driver's side. Once he was in, he crammed the key in the ignition and looked at me.

"You ready for the best date of your life?" he said, pulling the car from the spot.

"You're awfully sure of yourself, but I've had some pretty good dates. I mean, one guy did convince me to drive a car off into a lake."

"Pft. That guy is an idiot and obviously wasn't smart enough to keep you around."

"He was something," I said, focusing on a narrow dirt road winding through the trees. The exit was almost an exact replica of the main entrance, except more trees kept it hidden and it had a large cattle guard.

"You mean to tell me there's another entrance to this place and no one bothered to mention it?" I said. "I could've already snuck out a million times."

"Which is why the info is only reserved for privileged and experienced counselors like myself. Now that you know, you have to use it responsibly."

"Like for secret dates with my co-counselor?" I said.

"Yep."

Grant pulled the car through the gate. The dirt road blended with a long stretch of highway a few minutes later. Dimly lit, with little traffic, the two-lane country road had virtually no ending and no scenery but trees.

"So, what is this grand date plan of yours?" I said after a minute. "To get us lost in the woods, then apologize with Starbucks?"

"Would you like that?"

I tapped my fingers against my jaw, letting my attention

linger on the window. "I think that depends on how late this Starbucks is open."

"We'll go there first," he said, laughing. "You've been talking about it long enough I think you might rebel if I get us there *after* they've closed."

"Or I'll cry," I said.

"I thought you said you don't cry?"

"I'll cry for that."

He reached over and grabbed my hand, grinning as he steered us through the night. Deer scattered both sides of the road, a few threatening to make their way in front of us. Grant slowed for them, easing my nerves and getting us into Lufkin just after nine forty-five.

"We managed to get here with fifteen minutes to spare," he said, slowing at a stoplight. "Let's get the caffeine, then get to the real part of the date. I'm going to need a shot or two of espresso if we're going to be even remotely successful locating anything."

"Locating anything like . . ."

"Geocaches."

I arched a brow as he merged onto the loop. "Is there a description that comes with that word, or should I already know what that means?"

"You've never been geocaching?" he said, gawking at me from across the console.

"Nope. I've done a lot of things, but that isn't one of them."

"Then we're definitely going." He pulled his phone from the console, handing it to me. "Find the app that says geocache. I saved some of the coordinates earlier."

I took the phone from him, pausing at the picture on his phone screen. A selfie of what looked like a younger version of

Grant and the same man from the photo in Grant's cabin stared back at me. Same chestnut-colored hair. Same vivid hazel eyes. Same sharp facial features as the guy who sat across from me now.

"Is this you and your dad?" I said, scrolling through the apps.

"Yeah," he said, slowing as he exited the loop. "I think I was twelve in that picture. Maybe eleven. Can't remember exactly."

"Y'all look alike."

"Thanks. I hear that all the time."

I found the geocache app and hit it with my thumb. "So, in the interest of getting to know you better, where are you from?" I said.

"Why do you randomly want to know?" he asked.

"Thought it might be a good idea, given that this is a date and that's usually what people do."

"Boring people."

"So, Dallas?" I said. "One of those places in the Panhandle? You have an accent, so you have to be a born and bred Texan. I'm assuming somewhere in the backwoods."

"Um, you're the Cajun," Grant said, grinning. "And to answer your question, I currently live in Lubbock. I just finished my freshman year at Tech."

"What are you studying?"

"Sports management," he said. "Cliffs Notes: I'd eventually like to do some kind of sports-analyst job for ESPN. If it falls through, I'll probably aim for a sports-agent position or something along those lines."

"Sounds fun."

"For now," he said, shrugging. "But who knows? If my mom had it her way, I'd still be in Austin. She always saw me as getting into something more politically driven. Basketball analytics are the furthest thing from her idea of an interesting conversation topic."

"What about your dad? Who does he side with?"

"My dad died when I was thirteen. Hit by a drunk driver. But, if he was still around, I think he'd want me to do what makes me happy."

Nausea flooded my stomach, my fingers becoming increasingly heavy as I lifted a steely gaze. For as much as I could've curled into a tiny ball and shriveled into nothing, it was a good thing he was paying attention to pulling into Starbucks and wasn't focused on me.

"I'm sorry," I said. "I didn't—"

"Because we hadn't talked about it," Grant said. "But that's part of why we're on a date. You get to know me. I get to know you. That's how this works."

"Right." I returned my attention to the phone, my hands growing clammy as I pretended to focus on the locations Grant had marked under his favorites. Why hadn't he said anything?

"But that doesn't mean you have to get all awkward," he said, slowing in the drive-through. "Please don't get awkward."

"I'm not getting awkward," I said.

"I've been around you enough to read you," Grant said. He shifted, pulling his wallet from his back pocket. "I've just learned it's easier to get it out of the way. Before you go on thinking he's alive."

"I get it," I said, making a concerted effort to stare at the screen. "You don't have to explain."

Except I was single-handedly responsible for someone dying in a drinking and driving–related accident.

My arms shook and anxiety snaked its way up my spine as any appetite I'd had quickly disappeared. Any emotions I'd had were replaced by guilt and remorse, and the carnal urge to flee the situation. I needed to get out of here. I had to.

"What do you want to drink?" Grant said.

"Um, water."

He arched a brow, his hands becoming stock-still on the steering-wheel. "You want a water? After all those lively conversations about your love for Starbucks and their amazing iced coconut milk caramel macchiato?"

He let out a long sigh, staring at the menu again. "I have officially killed this date."

"You didn't," I said.

"Look me in the eye and say that again."

I lifted my gaze from the phone, meeting his unreadable expression. I was lying. He knew it. What was the point in pretending it wasn't true?

"You might be a master of sarcasm, but you're a terrible liar," he said, shaking his head.

"Yeah? Well, most people aren't as good at reading me as you seem to be."

The frown on his face and disappointment in his slumped shoulders tugged at my heartstrings. He couldn't know how one simple truth about his life would affect me, how it pulled memories of that night with Nikki to the forefront and flooded my mind with guilt.

I should've taken the keys, but I was too worried about getting caught by my dad to do the right thing. This was the consequence. It would always be the consequence.

"You haven't ruined the date," I said, lying to us both. "I

just . . . I know someone who died in kind of the same way and it just caught me off guard. It's easier to ignore those emotions."

"Welcome to Starbucks. What can I get you?" someone asked through the speaker.

Grant immediately shifted his attention to the menu, and I sat back in my chair heaving heavy breaths as he ordered my very specific coffee and a plain café Americano with an extra shot for him.

I'd dodged a bullet, but the sinking feeling in my gut told me I couldn't avoid the conversation forever. Somehow, someway, he'd find out about my involvement in Nikki's wreck. When and if he did, he'd never see me the same.

A few minutes later, amid an unexpected and unwanted tension, Grant pulled the car into a vacant Hobby Lobby parking lot. He stared out the window for a moment, silent.

"You can be totally honest with me and not hurt my feelings," he said, his voice barely above a whisper. "Do you want me to take you back to camp and chalk this date up to an epic failure on my part?"

"This date isn't an epic failure, and if I didn't want to be here, I wouldn't be," I said, looking at him.

"I brought up my dead dad in the Starbucks parking lot. I think that ranks up there with most horrible dates in the history of dating."

"You get brownie points for coffee," I said, forcing a sympathetic smile. "But, real talk, if you're wanting normal Alex, I need to focus on these geocaches and less on the serious stuff. I can't process it on my end, okay?"

"Are you at camp *to* process it?"

"I'm at camp to get away," I said. I handed him back his

phone. "So help me do that. Tell me what a geocache is and walk me through how to find it."

"You really want to know?"

"I really do."

Despite my completely unnerved stomach, I grabbed the coffee he ordered me and forced myself to take a sip. The liquid was sweet on my tongue, the extra caramel drizzle counteracting the bitterness of the cold brew.

"All right," he said, showing me the screen. "First things first, a geocache is a tiny little capsule people hide in random places."

"Like buried treasure?"

"Like pointless trinkets they happen to have on hand," he said. "There's supposed to be one in this parking lot called the *Magic 8 Ball*. It's described as a small tub with a Magic 8 Ball key chain in it, but we have to find the tub."

"Ideas on where to look?"

"I have a map," he said, flashing me the screen. "Well, the coordinates anyway, and a clue that makes zero sense."

I nodded, unbuckling my seat belt as he turned off the car and pulled the key from the ignition. On the feeder road, a handful of cars passed slowly. Goose bumps spread across my arms, the breeze chilling my skin more than the eeriness of being here after close.

"Something about this feels like we're breaking the law," I said, the parking lot crunching beneath my sandals.

"I would never take you on a date and expect you to break the law," Grant said, grinning at me as he extended his hand. "I'm pretty sure that would be a one-way ticket to pissing off your dad, and an even bigger way to piss off my mom. The governor's kid is supposed to be a law-abiding picture of perfection, not some recently redeemed delinquent who went and got himself arrested again."

I paused, pulling him back when he decided to continue walking. "I'm sorry. Did you say your mom is the governor?"

"Yes. And before you ask, no I can't get you out of a speeding ticket."

I studied him for a moment, quiet building between us.

"What?" he said, shifting his weight. "Were you really wanting me to get you out of a speeding ticket?"

"My dad's a cop. I don't need help getting out of them," I said. "I'm just wondering why you haven't said anything about your mom. That's a pretty important job to just leave out of a conversation."

"We haven't had a conversation where I needed to mention it."

His fingers brushed my cheek, the touch of his skin lighting my nerves. A guy with a family name to uphold was the furthest thing from what I needed to be around. For that matter, I was the furthest thing from what he needed too.

"You're being awkward again," he said. "And you're going to have to talk to me because I can't read your mind. What's going on in there?"

"A million different things, including but not limited to how I'm probably the bad influence in this relationship."

"Um, I'm the bad influence," he said. "I snuck us out tonight, remember?"

"Risking your pro-counselor status for a date with a girl you barely even know," I said. "Let's be real for a second. Okay? What would your mom say if she knew you were geocaching in Lufkin with me, when you were supposed to be monitoring a group of campers?"

"She'd applaud me for catching such an amazing girl," Grant said.

"I'm being serious."

"Fine. She'd probably ask me what I traded to get the night off, then she'd commend me for my expert negotiating skills. Why? What would your dad say?"

"How irresponsible it is that I willingly snuck out of camp when I'm supposed to be here fixing myself," I said.

"You're fine the way you are."

"You don't know me," I said.

"I know you well enough." Grant tucked a piece of hair behind my ear, kissing me lightly. "And I happen to like the girl you are," he muttered against my lips. "Bad decisions and everything."

"What happens when these bad decisions get both of us in trouble?" I said, pulling pulled his lip between my teeth.

"I don't know. Maybe we won't have to find out."

He kissed me again, his body shielding us from the rest of the world as he backed me against the car. His hands, strong and calloused, cradled my face while his mouth slanted over mine and kissed me with an intensity that could've melted me into the metal.

My body was on fire, my hands sliding up his shoulder blades while the intoxicating smell of his body wash wound its way through my senses. Every piece of attraction I couldn't show at camp was free for the taking. Whoever he was, or whoever he wasn't, didn't matter. He was Grant. I was Alex.

In that moment, that's all that mattered.

15

Honest

"Well, someone seems happy," Madeline said, catching me the next morning.

After one hell of a date with Grant, followed by one sleepless night thinking up every reason why the pair of us couldn't work, Loraine's stupid therapy schedule *would* swoop in and wreck my day. Figures.

"It's my cabin's day to sweep out the pavilion and squeegee the floors," I said, glancing at Madeline. "How about we skip today's round of therapy and pretend like we had it?"

"Except Loraine gets a copy of all my notes," Madeline said. "If we skip, she'll wonder where all my assessment pages have disappeared to."

"Hold up," I said, the words spurring immediate annoyance. "I thought if you shared what we talked about in these sessions it was a violation of client privilege. Is that an actual law, or is it just something my parents made up to keep me plugging away at therapy back home?"

"Back home it's different. Here, you're in a gray area where you're not legally considered a client. It's in the welcome manual."

"I didn't get a damn welcome manual," I said, rolling my eyes. I kicked a rock, bypassing my cabin for the gazebo. If we had to do this, we needed to get it out of the way before my girls realized I was gone.

We found our usual therapy setting a few minutes later, the lack of campers around it typical of morning time.

"You've got all of twenty minutes," I said, tapping my wrist with my finger. "I'm out of here after that. You can just write in your notes how I said *f-you* and walked my happy little butt out of here."

"Still hostile," Madeline said.

"Still annoying."

She took a seat on the bench, flipping through her notebook with a smile. "All right," she said, clicking her pen. "The last time we chatted, you were explaining to me how your at-home therapist is, and I quote, 'the most boring human on the face of the earth.' Would you like to continue with that conversation, or do you have something else you'd like to talk about?"

I weighed the decision, my hands drumming absently against the gazebo's wooden backing. In a plain green tee and blue-jean shorts, Madeline's casual clothing and persistent smile made her way more welcoming than Dr. Heichman could ever hope to be. Maybe she *could* be the one to let me word vomit all the issues spiraling around my head.

As it stood, mine and Grant's situation would end one of two ways: Either I would tell Grant the truth about Nikki and he'd judge me, confirming that everyone I let in always eventually left. Or his mom would get wind of my rap sheet and judge me hard enough I wouldn't be comfortable staying with him anyway. What respectable politician would okay their son being with someone like me? None.

There was no happy ending. At least not one I could see.

"Alex," Madeline said, tilting her head into view. "I can't start our session time until you answer my first question. You're obligated for at least thirty minutes."

"That's a stupid rule."

"It's Loraine's rule, and as her employee I have to abide by it," Madeline said. "So, what would you like to talk about? Dr. Heichman? How bored you are at camp? How the mosquitoes are tiny little raptors?"

I paused for a minute, picking at a loose string on my shorts. "Is there any way we could talk *off* the record?" I said. "Like, you could just start the timer and I could talk to you about whatever, without you relaying the information to Loraine?"

"I have to turn in my notes," Madeline said.

"Why?"

"Rules."

I pulled my lip between my teeth as an overwhelming sense of anxiety flooded my vision. I would work this out on my own before I let Loraine catch wind of it. She'd turn around and report everything to my parents. Then they'd take it and leverage it against the college fund I was already trying to prove I deserved. I didn't need them sticking their noses in a complicated situation they had no part of, and I definitely didn't need Loraine doing it.

Things were hard as it was.

Madeline tapped her pen against her notebook, her eyes hidden behind large retro-style sunglasses. From my vantage point, she seemed to be analyzing me with a magnifying glass, mentally surveying my responses before she summarized them and crammed them in her notebook.

"Never mind," I said. "It was a stupid question."

I crossed my arms and relaxed into my seat, my position firmly cemented on this side of silence.

Madeline frowned, her pen stopping. "You're more than welcome to tell me whatever it is you wanted to say."

Silence.

"I don't have to jot down *every* piece of our conversation," she said.

Silence.

This brick wall of resolve wouldn't budge from now until the time I walked out of this camp. Had I realized everything was getting reported to Loraine in the first place, I would've shut up sooner and left both of them in the dark.

Madeline sighed and put her pen down, closing the notebook on her lap. "You can speak to me openly," she said. "It's my decision to choose what I do and don't see fit to disclose to your aunt."

"Just like it's my decision to choose what I do and don't disclose to you," I said.

"Do you always push back when people are honest with you, or is this another one of the masks you use to hide disappointment and confliction?"

"You're the therapist. You tell me."

"I feel like it's your go-to for deflection of emotion," Madeline said. "You create an unmovable wall between others and yourself, hoping they'll give up and surrender to your inability to compromise."

"I was willing to compromise and talk to you, under the agreement you wouldn't take notes. You weren't willing to meet me halfway, so I'm not talking. How is that deflecting my emotions?"

"You tell me," she said.

My brow furrowed as the stranger in front of me grew more frustrating by the second. She didn't know me. She knew absolutely nothing about me. Unless . . .

"You said you give your notes to my aunt after each session," I said. "Why?"

"So she can keep a running record of your progress while you're here."

"What for?"

"I think you know," Madeline said. She pulled her glasses from her face, her dark brown eyes surveying me from where she sat. Accusation sat within them, mixed with a tinge of sympathy that left me on edge.

"Ask yourself what the primary reason for Loraine scheduling these sessions would be, then apply it to yourself. What is it you need to work on most? What issue or issues have driven you to a point in life where you find yourself here?"

"I'm here because my parents forced me to be here," I said. "Because if I didn't agree to come either here or to boarding school, they'd withhold a college fund that is rightfully mine."

"Why would they withhold it?"

"I don't know, Madeline. Why don't you call them and ask?"

She shook her head, a small smile playing at her lips. "You're back to deflection, Alex. Take a moment and recognize that behavior. Based on the tone in your voice, I believe what you're feeling lies somewhere between anger and annoyance."

"This is stupid," I groaned.

"Answer my question and we'll proceed."

I pinched the bridge of my nose, my attention shifting to a tiny trail of ants making their way across the gazebo's concrete floor. It must be a requirement for therapists to take a crash course in how to piss people off. Both Madeline and Dr. Heichman were experts at it.

"Why would they withhold a college fund that is rightfully yours?" she said.

"Because I failed my last year of high school, so now they think I can't make good decisions," I said, glaring at her. "There. Happy?"

"Have you made poor decisions before?"

"Have *you* made poor decisions before?" I snapped.

She paused, an emotionless mask pasted to her face. She wasn't giving me anything in regard to response. At least Dr. Heichman got frazzled from time to time. This woman was a stone-wall. My inability to get a rise out of her frustrated me more.

"Based on what your aunt has disclosed, I would assume you've—"

"I've made one or two bad decisions," I said, cutting her off. "I'm human. I never claimed to be perfect. I never wanted to be perfect."

"No one is perfect, Alex."

I pulled my lip between my teeth, my heart pounding as my conversation with Grant replayed through my mind. No. No one was perfect. Especially someone who would allow something so heinous to happen to someone she cared about.

"In your lifetime, you're allowed to make the wrong choice. That's what living is. It's a series of complicated decisions and our ability to weave through them, doing the best we can to pick the right path along the way. But I think where you're getting hung up on your progress is in thinking that people want perfection from you, when in reality they just want you to be okay. Your aunt, and I'm sure your parents, are just legitimately concerned for your well-being."

I swallowed, the words slicing through me like a knife.

"And they don't think you've internalized all the grieving emotions you needed to. You haven't moved on, Alex. You're stuck in a self-loathing mentality that's breaking you down mentally and emotionally, and you either don't see it or won't accept it."

"How am I supposed to accept it?" I said, staring at her. "How do I go back to normal when my life is everything *but* normal?"

"You take it day by day and do the best you can."

"And what about everyone else?" I said. "You want me to move on? Okay. Tell me how I do that when the decision I made destroyed a family. *My* decision ruined people's lives. I can't just swallow the guilt and move on. I can't take it day by day. I can't take it at all! You want me to grieve and get over it but you don't understand. No one understands."

I stood, cramming my hands in my pockets. Sitting was like keeping myself under a current, like trying to breathe while a riptide held me under.

"You're fleeing," Madeline said, standing too. "Stay here and talk about this with me."

"I don't have to."

I exited beneath the gazebo's low-slung rafters, taking a

deep breath as midmorning heat hit my cheeks. The grass, still drying from the morning dew, clung to my bare legs as I walked toward my cabin.

I spotted Grant along the way, hauling a set of floats from the storage shed beside the camp office. In this world of complicated choices, where one wrong decision could affect so much, someone's decision to drink and drive left him fatherless. Forever changed. Scarred.

And I was the reverse. The guilty. The villain for letting someone too intoxicated to think get behind the wheel.

The minute he knew, he would look at me differently. The minute he knew, he would want someone else.

* * *

Later that afternoon, after a long duty shift at arts and crafts failed to get my mind off every terrible thought spiraling through it, I bypassed the mess hall and headed straight for the junction. As the only food provider aside from the mess hall, campers flocked to The Hut from one to five. Kira sat behind the glass window, grinning as I neared.

"If this is where you tell me you're here to save me from an impossibly boring second shift, I will literally cry tears of joy," she said.

I leaned against the building's side paneling, eyeing the crowd. "I don't think I have the patience to handle this many people," I said, shaking my head. "But I would be happy to keep you company."

"The door is in the back," she said.

I walked the rest of the way around the building and found the small metal doorknob at the back. Inside, popcorn popped in the cooker. The smell of butter was strong, but not as strong as the smell of hot dogs spinning to my right. Gross.

"I couldn't last more than an hour in here," I said, scrunching my nose. "Could be the smell of processed mystery meat. I don't know."

"Trust me, if I could've smooth talked my way out of doing this I would've. Better yet, I should've made Grant do it. He owes me for covering for y'all last night."

My stomach did a somersault. I was trying to escape Grant. Or, at least, trying to escape the guilt and anxiety that came with him.

"How did it go, anyway?" she said. "Haven't seen either of you that much today."

"I tried to stop by after breakfast but was forced to do something else instead," I said.

"Well, we had an issue with the guys' side and Linc ended up needing me to cover his yoga session so I wouldn't have been there anyway. I swear, watching those kids try to do yoga was hilarious but annoying. There was more complaining than anything. They would've rather been swimming. Can't say I blame them."

I took a seat on the stool beside her. Her brown eyes wore dark bags beneath them. I probably looked the same, except mine were from a lack of sleep and too many thoughts flooding my mind.

"Sooo, how was the date?" Kira said. "Awesome? Fantastic? The best first date in the history of mankind?"

"We got Starbucks and went geocaching."

"Sounds fun."

"Yeah," I said.

Kira paused, eyeing me as she took a punch card from a kid outside The Hut. Clearly the lack of enthusiasm in the answer wasn't what she expected to hear.

I shifted beneath her scrutinizing stare. "I had a good time," I said.

"Because you *sound* like you had a good time," she said, standing from her stool. "Girl, I know an issue when I see it. Spill it. Was he not what you expected him to be?"

"Grant was fine," I said, shaking my head.

"Then what's the problem here? Lack of chemistry outside of camp? Boring conversations? His crappy sense of humor?"

"I like his humor."

"But you don't like him?"

"I do."

I took the punch card from the next kid, making a concerted effort to look anywhere but at Kira, who was burning holes in my profile.

"I'm the one on duty shift," she said, bringing a Dr Pepper to the window. "And you're doing a terrible job answering questions. What's the deal? Judgment-free zone. Talk all you want."

"I came here for a distraction. Not another round of therapy."

"Let's be clear. I'm nothing like Madeline. Who, since you brought it up, shouldn't be seeing you anyway."

Halfway through opening the rancid hot-dog spinner, I froze.

"Not that it's my business," Kira said, holding up a hand. "I'm just saying, people noticed the pair of you having your conversations in the gazebo. Theories are going round. Some think it has to do with that cop-car thing the campers were talking about, but I think it's Loraine trying to butt into your business."

"Definitely the second," I said, irritation sparking at the

mention of what was supposed to be a confidential conversation between me and my girls.

"And I'd really appreciate it if everyone would quit talking about the cop-car thing," I said. "I told my campers about that because I thought it would help them see me as something other than a counselor, but clearly I was wrong in trusting them not to open their mouths. Geez. I thought Grant squashed it."

"He might have in *his cabin*," Kira said. "But he can't control everybody. His family doesn't have that much control."

"Yeah, he told me about his family," I said, sucking in a breath. "Including the part about his mom being the governor, which everybody failed to mention to me."

"Does it really make a difference?"

"It does when you've already got enough on your plate," I said. I grabbed a bun and crammed a hot dog in it. "I mean, it would've at least been nice to know. It kind of complicates things, considering I'm clearly a delinquent and his mom is apparently the perfection of the law. At least I'm assuming. If she wasn't, she wouldn't be the governor."

"I don't know. In today's world, all sorts of people get elected to things they may or may not be qualified to do. Regardless, it's not like Grant hasn't screwed up a time or two. He went off the deep end after his dad died. Theft. Burglary. Controlled-substance charges. He was a totally different person when he came out here and now he's *Grant*."

Theft. Burglary. Controlled substances.

What else didn't I know about him?

"The point is, people change," Kira said. "His mom can sit there and judge you all she wants, but people mess up. That's life."

"People don't just mess up," I said. "They make choices that are selfish. His dad died in a wreck that could've been prevented. If someone would've taken two seconds and just—"

A knot formed in the base of my throat, killing the sentence with emotion I was fighting to bury.

If someone would've just taken the keys, I wanted to say, but my guilt was already swallowing me. I hadn't done that. How could I pass judgment on someone else for the same crime?

I swallowed thickly and took a staggered breath as I finished the hot dog and carried it to the window. The camper outside, with her brown eyes and hair the same shade of red as Nikki's, crumbled my resolve.

Tears burned my eyes. This was the beginning of the end. Either I could kill the emotions, or they *would* kill me. That's how I survived. That's how I always survived.

"I can't," I said.

I bypassed Kira, opening the door to a staggering afternoon heat that did nothing to warm the chill in my bones. Thinking I was capable of an actual relationship was the first mistake. Everyone I loved always left. Grant would be just another name to add to the list. Not that I blamed him. He deserved more. So much more.

Emotions piled with each passing step, curling my stomach and winding dread through every inch of me. Minutes later, I exited the line of trees. A diving board sounded behind the pool's large concrete wall. Voices echoed from inside, ricocheting off the walls with splashes of water between their words.

This wasn't the right place, and it wasn't the right time, but it had to happen. I had to squash everything before either of us was in too deep to get out. It was the only thing I could do.

Through the pool's opening, the crowd of campers gathered in the water was thicker than the voices would imply. They dripped water across the concrete, padding barefoot to and around large folding chairs on either side of the pool. Brie was lounging on one of them, her position the same one as the day she and Jess skipped yoga.

She didn't even look my way. With her eyes closed and her hands by her side, she drank in the sunlight a mere three feet from where Grant sat atop his perch.

He glanced my way, his eyes hidden by a pair of aviator sunglasses. The smile on his face, full of excitement and deepening the single dimple in his right cheek, made my anxiety flare. He was so handsome. So charming. Out of my league in too many ways, but gorgeous just the same.

And he had no idea of the complications one simple statement could bring.

"Hey," he said, climbing off the perch. "Didn't expect to see you here, but I can't say I'm mad about it. You swimming?"

I shook my head, glancing at the group of campers splashing their way through the afternoon. "No, I finished my shift at arts and crafts and thought I would visit with Kira for a little bit."

"Gotcha," he said. "I think she's in the hut. She doesn't come out here unless she has to. Most of the time Linc does it for her instead."

"Except for today."

"Except for today," Grant said. "Since I stupidly agreed to cover his shift in exchange for our date. You were totally worth it, but I'm roasting out here. It's like no matter how much sunblock I put on, the sun keeps getting hotter and hotter and—"

"It's not the sun," Brie mumbled. "It's you. *All* you."

"Oh, and I'm also dealing with that one," Grant said, putting his hands on either side of his hips. "I think she enjoys making me uncomfortable."

"You mean that's possible?" I said, staring at him. "I thought you had a three-second rebound rate. You could throw anything out there and all it would do is bounce back with a vengeance."

"That's called wit," he said. "Which I also have a ton of."

"Humble."

"The humblest," he said. He shifted the weight on his feet. "I haven't seen you much today. You been hiding?"

"Figured I would spare both of us the awkward morning-after conversation, where we either pretend like the date didn't happen or beat around the bush until someone brings it up," I said. "I'm never good with that kind of stuff."

"Same," he said. "I know I come across as someone who *might* know what they're doing when it comes to this kind of thing, but I know nothing. I'm an awkward duck in an appealing package."

His hand moved to the brim of his hat, adjusting it slightly. "But, since neither of us is hiding, and we're already on the topic, I had a good time with you last night. Outside of you losing the 8 Ball from the Hobby Lobby geocache."

"In my defense, it was tiny, and I didn't realize I wasn't supposed to take it," I said. "I thought everyone got their own little trinket. That's how you described it."

"No, I said *we* could take one thing out of the geocache. I didn't mean you and me individually."

"You should've specified."

"Or you should've read between the lines."

"Or you should've known me well enough to know I need

step-by-step directions if you want me to do anything remotely related to following the rules," I said.

He pointed at me, his mouth ajar.

"And you know I'm right, which is why you have zero comeback lines," I said, crossing my arms.

He shook his head, lowering his hand so it grazed mine. Warmth flooded my cheeks. The reason for me coming here in the first place was to end everything going on between us, but how could I when being around him was so easy?

"8 Ball aside, I had a good time with you," he said. "Unless you're about to serve me a shot of reality, I'm pretty sure you did too. But who knows? You aren't known for your tact."

"Tact? What's that?"

"It's a trait some people have, where they don't spit out the first thing on their mind. Instead, they stop to consider the other person's feelings. Or so I've heard. Never tried it."

"You two done flirting over there?" Brie said behind us, her voice annoying as nails on a chalkboard.

"Nope," I said.

She let out a long sigh and sat up, scowling as she opened both eyes. "Well, then do me a favor and at least consider your campers the next time you two go on an adventure. I mean, I was stuck in that boring cabin while you two were geocaching. What is life?"

"Tough," Grant said, staring at her.

"Tougher when she gets assigned to scrub our toilets during tomorrow morning's chore time," I said.

"Ugh. Whatever," Brie said, rolling her eyes. She closed them again, returning to her former position on the folding chair.

Grant stared at her a moment, scowling as he returned his

attention to me. "I know I said all campers need someone to relate to, but geez. How do you tolerate that one? She annoys *me* and I'm used to it."

"Meh, she's not that bad when she's got Jess around to keep her in check."

"Um, I keep Jess in check," Brie said.

"Anyway," Grant said, ignoring her. "So you and me are good? No weirdness? No deciding you're really not into me?"

"I mean, I was never *into* you. You just kind of annoyed me until I had to pay attention to you," I said.

"Same," Grant said, grinning. "We'll just continue annoying the crap out of each other until we either can't stand one another or we can't stand to be without the other. Which ought to be fun either way."

And complicated.

"Oh!" he said, snapping his fingers. "That reminds me! I have this top-secret assignment I was hoping to hit you up on. If the thought of being around me more than you have to be doesn't seem like something that would make you want to get lost in the woods again."

"I wasn't lost. I was just looking for my way out," I said.

"You were sitting on the ground, pouting."

"Tomato. To-mah-to. What's the assignment? Let's focus on that."

"Camper talent show," he said. "The midsession event that sends all the campers scouring for hidden talents. Everyone wants to participate, but only the strong survive."

"So they battle to the death?"

"What kind of organizer do you think I am? Clearly they go three rounds."

I quirked an eyebrow.

"Three rounds of auditions," he said. "We start off with a big net, narrow it down to fifteen, then narrow it down to ten. The counselors also organize a skit, and most of the camp admin staff does something too. We'd be in charge of narrowing the list."

"You mean I get to be Simon Cowell for a day?" I said.

"Yeah, and when you're not crushing the hopes and dreams of people auditioning, you get to spend time with me. It's a win-win."

"Alone time?"

"You think I'd offer this side job to just anyone?" he said, putting his hand in front of his heart. "No. This is an Alex kind of job. No other counselor could hack it."

While the camper talent show seemed far from fun, spending unchaperoned time with Grant was hard to turn down. Then again, I should turn it down. Finding more time with him was just another way to dig a deeper hole for myself.

I was already in too deep.

"You know, I think I'm actually going to sit this out," I said, stepping backward. "Thanks for the offer though."

"Whoa, whoa, whoa," Grant said, keeping a hold on my hand. "What happened in the last two seconds that sent you from serious contemplation to *no not interested*? I feel like I missed something."

"It's too vanilla for me."

"Too vanilla? Do you think I do *vanilla*?"

I surveyed him, the smile in his face dying as seconds ticked by.

"I've adjusted to this whole counselor thing, but I'm just not interested in helping with a talent show," I said. "Even if you're included."

Despite his eyes being covered by the aviators, Grant's furrowed brow and slightly pursed lips told me enough of what he was thinking. He was either annoyed, confused, or both.

"But I appreciate the offer," I said.

"Right. Okay." He cleared his throat, taking a step backward. "Noted."

I pushed a piece of hair behind my ear and stared at the pool for the millionth time, because pretending to watch the campers was way easier than facing him straight on.

"I think I'm going to get back on my perch now, where the sting of rejection is easier to deal with."

"I'm not rejecting you," I said, an unmistakable tension forming between us. "I'm rejecting the talent show."

"Got it," he said. "You have the right to say no, and you did that. I guess I just wasn't really expecting it."

"Grant."

"Let's just pause the conversation," he said. "For when there aren't a bunch of campers floating around, eavesdropping. Later?"

"Yeah."

I stepped away, crossing through the opening in the pool's concrete wall while echoes of the conversation rang through my mind. Rejection was the only real way of keeping myself safe, but Grant had no clue what he did wrong.

He couldn't know. He never would.

16

Fate

Around nine forty-five, I dragged a hoodie from beneath my bed and hauled it over my head. The girls were playing a game of Monopoly near the cabin door. Brie held the dice as I passed. Her eyes landed on my hoodie for a second, her eyebrow arching.

"You can't seriously be going out on a date for the second night in a row," she said. "I mean, how is it fair that you get action and we're stuck in this cabin playing some hokey board game?"

"What she means to say is: If you're meeting Grant again, could you at least get us some food from the mess hall?" Jess said, nudging her friend. "I would prefer leftover brownies, if possible."

"Or a jar of those dill pickles they set out when it's hoagie day," Steff said, glancing at me. "Those are amazing."

"But brownies if you can only pick one," Jess said.

"I'll do what I can," I said, quietly opening the cabin door.

Outside, a warm night breeze riffled loose strands of hair. I had made a concerted effort to avoid Grant the rest of the afternoon, but my emotions were in a tailspin.

How could I shut him down, when I cared about him? When the only thing I wanted to do was spend time with him? But how could I not let him go? How could I knowingly let this continue when my own demons were gnawing away at my conscience? When he thought he knew the real version of me but really had no clue?

No. In the end, this would be the best thing for both of us. I could detach before he had the chance to hurt me. He could do the same.

Inside Grant's side of the cabin, the strum of his guitar drifted through the screen door. He was playing what sounded like an acoustic version of James Arthur's "Empty Space." It was hard to tell, though, with guys talking around him and the rhythm too muddled to hear.

I leaned against the porch, drinking in the dark. This time of night, stripped of campers and chaos, was the most peaceful. A stillness clung to the air, chilling despite the chaos of the day.

Releasing a breath, I stared down the opposite end of the road. A flashlight bobbed up and down in the dark, and I heard tennis shoes crunching against the path. The closer she got, the more defined Loraine's face became.

"Are you doing cabin patrols?" I said, surveying her.

"No, but we need to talk."

Dread curled up my spine. The tone in her voice walked a fine line between frustration and disappointment. Her expression was a mirror image of my mom's when she was pissed. That told me everything I needed to know—we had a problem, and I didn't know what it was.

I pulled away from the rail, mentally prepping myself for conflict. "Is this the part where you tell me I'm in trouble?" I said, stepping off the porch. "You sound like my mom, so I'm guessing *yes*."

"I'd rather talk about this in private," she said, pivoting the other direction.

I let out a long sigh. Another serious conversation was the last thing I needed at this exact moment. My plate was full. Full of worry. Full of chaos. Full of guilt.

"If you're about to yell at me, it really doesn't matter where you do it," I said. "Just spit it out. What did I do and how do I fix it?"

"Madeline turned in your therapy notes today and I was looking over them when I realized you walked out of today's session *five* minutes into it. Those sessions aren't optional," Loraine said, facing me. "They're a part of the deal, remember?"

"A deal I didn't realize I was agreeing to when I got here," I said, stopping. "You threw that part in *after* I was already settled. I never would've agreed had I known."

"But you did agree and here we are. You're skipping out on sessions, and I'm the one who has to explain to your parents why you've been out here almost a month and haven't made any serious headway with the person I told them was the best juvenile counselor this side of Houston."

"Because as far as I'm concerned, none of my emotions or reactions or thoughts for that matter are anyone's business," I said. "I'll end those sessions when I damn well want to, and if you don't like it you can cancel them altogether."

"Did you just swear at me?"

"Damn. Damn. Damn," I said, putting my hands on my hips. "Why? Have I broken another cardinal rule of camp?"

"You're about to get yourself written up."

"Then quit lecturing me on how long I am or am not in therapy with a therapist *I didn't ask for!*"

I glared at her, my temper flaring the longer she stood unmoving. How dare she expect me to talk to a stranger about my feelings? That had nothing to do with her. That had nothing to do with anyone but me and it was *my* decision.

"As long as you're out here, you'll abide by my rules," Loraine said.

"I didn't even want to come out here," I said. "And if me opening up to some crappy counselor isn't a negotiable, then you're either going to have to kick me out or you're going to have to get over it. *I'm* the one who gets to open up to people when I feel like it, so walking out of a therapy session is my choice. Not yours. Not my parents'. Mine."

Her lips formed a thin line in the dark. Her shoulders turned rigid.

"Y'all didn't even ask me what I wanted," I said. "You and everyone else just thought they could pick and choose what's best for me, but no one bothered to ask! No one *ever* asks!"

I shook my head, crossing my arms as heat flooded my cheeks. With the events of the day and the stress of what I had to do with Grant boiling already, I couldn't handle this. It was too much.

"You and I both know everyone is just concerned for your well-being," Loraine said. "You've been through a lot, Alex. You've seen way more than you ever should. That affects a person."

"I know!" I said, throwing my hands up. "I was there! I lived it. *I* was the one trying to make it through my last year of school. *I* was the one trying to figure out how to live in a world where my best friend no longer existed. *I* was the one—"

Grief formed a knot at the base of my throat. I would choke on those words before I said them out loud. Before I ever admitted to anyone that *I* was to blame for Nikki. That *I* could've taken the keys.

Tears burned my eyes; emotion spiraled its way through me.

All these months and I had kept this to myself. I drowned in the guilt and internalized how I felt about it so no one would judge me for not doing more to save my friend, so I wouldn't have to live with people knowing I could've changed the outcome but chose to be selfish instead.

But here I was, standing in some horrible reformation camp, giving it the exact same thing it wanted from me. Admission. Guilt. Acceptance of my faults and everything that came with it.

And I couldn't do it. I couldn't say it was my fault.

"Is everything okay?" Grant said from behind me.

His voice, so full of conviction, broke the last of what little resolve I was using to hold myself together. Tears burned their way across my cheeks. My guilt swallowing me whole.

"I can't do this," I said, stepping away. "I can't. You. Him. I want to go home."

"No!" Loraine said, shaking her head. "You have to quit holding on to all these emotions and just grieve, Alex. Quit running away. Quit being so stubborn and let us help you. Please."

"How are *you* going to help me?" I said, facing her. "You have no idea what I've been through. You have no idea what I'm feeling. I lost my friend, Loraine. Someone who knew and accepted me long before anyone else ever did. Who saw me. The real me, and liked me anyway. You have no idea what it's like to lose someone like that. You have no idea."

"I do," Grant said.

I closed my eyes, tears hot on my cheeks.

"I know exactly how that feels. I lost my best friend. My role model. My hero. And I don't know how that played out for you, but I spiraled. I spiraled *hard*. Don't do that. Not when you have people willing and ready to help you. Not when they *want* to help you."

"So what happens when they realize *you're* the one responsible for your own destruction?" I said, my body shaking as I forced the sentences out. "What happens when you have to explain to the people who have this huge faith in you that you're the one who let your friend keep the keys? That you knew they were drunk and you let them drive anyway?"

The pair of them froze, the words a wall between us.

"You're blinded by your faith in me," I said, shaking my head. "You want to preach at me about how I can help myself. You want me to let it all out so I can move on. But I can't move on. I can't let it go. I have to live with this. And that's something you could never understand. I'm on my own. Quit trying to help me."

Silence filled the space as I headed for the dark, my admission breaking me down.

I was the one responsible for my fate. Now I had to live with it.

17

Flawed

The next morning, Grant wasn't on the porch.

He wasn't at breakfast.

He wasn't at lunch.

I crossed in front of cabin two, headed for a duty shift at arts and crafts. I needed to paint like I needed to breathe. It was the only way to channel these emotions into something beautiful. It was my first step in burying my grief.

Inside arts and crafts, campers clustered around each of the rectangular tables. Jess was at one of them, working on a bracelet. She glanced my way as I crossed the room, her attention returning to her bracelet as I approached the counselor on shift.

"Now that you're here, could I possibly . . ." The girl jabbed her finger toward the back where the bathrooms was.

"Absolutely," I said with a nod.

She scurried off and I turned toward the paint products.

I was carefully putting paint supplies on the countertop when Jess crossed the room, long pieces of string clutched between her finger and her thumb.

"All right," she said, dropping onto one of the bar stools. "Will you please explain to me what I'm doing wrong? I'm alternating the strings and everything, but this bracelet looks like crap."

"It doesn't look that bad," I said, surveying the knotted pieces of string that looked more like a chaotic heap than a bracelet.

"Yeah. You're a terrible liar."

"Only sometimes." I finished gathering supplies and stared at her. "That isn't really my thing anyway. I'm a painter, not a weaver."

"I'm neither, and Brie will rag me about it if I don't make her a bracelet after she spent all that time working on mine."

"Brie made you a bracelet?"

"She made four," Jess said. "One for her, and one for each of the girls in our cabin."

Surprised, I grabbed a canvas and laid it flat on the counter. For Brie to do anything selfless must have meant hell froze over. Or pigs flew. No telling which.

"I'll try," I said. "Step one would be to get you some fresh string. Pick out the colors you want. I'll give them to you for free."

"Thank you," Jess said, sliding off the stool.

I started sketching while she snipped pieces of yarn from the spools. When she returned, she plopped right onto the same bar stool and knotted the ends.

"What are you working on?" she asked after a second. "You haven't sketched enough to really make it out."

"I'm not sure," I said, tapping the pencil against my jaw. "Whatever the canvas wants to give me, I guess. Usually the picture creates itself. It never does what I want it to do."

"That's weird."

"That's me," I said.

I dragged the pencil across the canvas again, the charcoal tip marring its clean surface. If this ended up being any reflection of my state of mind, the final product would be dark and gloomy.

"I wish I could do that," Jess said after a moment. "I've got all this street cred and zero usable abilities. It's a shame, since talents like yours are the talents people actually appreciate."

The words stole my attention from the canvas, the disappointment in her tone making me pause. "Not everyone's talent is artistic," I said. "You, for example, could probably talk your way out of a paper bag. That's a talent, Jess."

"Meh. Anyone with half the experience I have could do the same."

"Doubt it."

She quirked an eyebrow and I set down my pencil, realizing I had unknowingly walked into a conversation.

"Okay," I said, leaning forward. "Remember when I told you about my tiny brush with the law?"

"You crashed a cop car into a lake," Jess said. "That isn't tiny."

"That doesn't matter. Point is, you could've talked your way out of that in five seconds flat. All I could do was sit in the back of a deputy's squad car, claiming I had nothing to do with it when my cell phone and purse were still inside the vehicle."

"Still not a talent. All my bullshitting has ever done is land me in a new group home with a new set of issues. Painting seems less dramatic and less of a hassle. I want *those* skills. I'll trade you."

"You live in a group home?" I said.

"Yeah," she said. "Right now, I'm technically a ward of the state. Unless I get adopted between now and the time I turn eighteen, which is doubtful. No one ever wants someone above the age of ten."

Guilt worked its way into my thoughts, pulling my attention back to the canvas. Had I known this earlier, I could have been softer from the beginning. Had I been softer, though, we may not have made it this far.

"You don't have to get all weird," she said. "You can look at me. I'm not asking for your sympathy or anything."

"No sympathy," I said, nodding. "I just didn't know. That caught me off guard."

"Well it isn't like I wore it around my neck on some flashing neon sign," Jess said. "Most people find out and they look at you some kind of way, like they want to help you but they don't know how, so they just avoid you instead."

"I can't avoid you. You're stuck with me."

"Exactly. You're stuck with me either way."

She went back to crisscrossing strings on the bracelet, making some sort of pattern as each of the strings worked together. After her fourth round of alternating, she looked at me.

"So, now that I've been all open and honest with you, do you feel like telling me what all that crying you were doing in your bed last night was about? I'm not here just to make a bracelet, Alex. If you're out here to be my counselor, you need to make sure that trust is flowing both ways."

"The last time I told y'all something, it ended up being passed around camp," I said.

"The last time you told us something, Brie was around. You should've expected it to be passed around camp."

I gave her the side-eye, focusing on my canvas instead of talking. She might understand, or she might not, but I wasn't talking about it anymore. Period.

"Okay," she said after a minute. "Talking isn't on the table. Got it. How about we break some rules instead? You give me the chance to do something fun, and I give you the chance to get your mind off your issues. At least temporarily."

"What do you want me to do? Sneak you out of camp?"

"Your suggestion. Not mine."

"You and I both know if I got you out of camp, Loraine would get me a one-way ticket home. I have a reason for being out here that revolves around a large sum of money and a set of parents who are already positive I can't make good choices. That's like confirming it."

"Your parents are that bad?"

"Well, they offered me an ultimatum to get me out here, then volunteered me for extra therapy sessions I never agreed to. At this point, I'm not even sure I want to go home. The longer I'm gone, the more I think I like being on my own."

"No one is better on their own."

"You haven't met my parents."

"At least you have parents."

I ran my tongue across my teeth, my jaw jutting to the side. Jess's expression was unflinching, her brown eyes squarely centered on mine. Leave it to a camper to attempt to put me in my place. Leave it to a camper to do the best job at it.

"Give me something real to go on here," she said.

"I'm not giving you anything but the free string you've already got."

"Then stand on your side of the counter and angrily draw something," she said. "Staying silent never changes anything, but you do you, boo."

"You're getting on my nerves."

"You always get on my nerves, but I never say anything to you," she said. She started on her bracelet again. "So was that the issue between you and Grant? Your annoying personality?"

"My issue with Grant is that he deserves someone better than me," I said, resting my hands on either side of the canvas. "And my current issue is that you won't get off the subject. What is it with the people at this camp? Geez. You're all nosy."

"Um, we spend the majority of our time doing stupid team-building exercises and expressing how we feel with people we don't really care to share it with," Jess said. "Excuse me for thinking maybe for once you'd feel like sharing something too."

"I have shared. Cop-car story. Remember?"

"Okay, and I just gave you deets on something personal. Does that mean I don't have to participate in any other summer activities? No. I'm stuck in yoga sessions, even though I don't want to be. Let me out of those and I'll let you out of this."

I rolled my eyes.

"Why do you think Grant deserves more than you?" Jess said. "Because he's way better-looking or because he's obviously more talented?"

"You're making me feel better by the second."

"My job isn't to make you feel better. It's to make myself a better human being, while trying to survive a summer at the dumbest camp in Texas," Jess said. "Back to the subject. You and Grant. What gives?"

"I thought I said I wasn't talking about this."

"Well, you've got another two hours in this shift. Trust me when I say I can sit here and badger you about it until you talk, or you can willingly talk about it now," she said. "A conversation won't kill you."

"Why the sudden interest in my life?"

"You kept me up until four a.m., lying over there sniffling all night," Jess said. "You weren't considerate enough to take your moping somewhere else, so I'm not going to be considerate enough to take my questions somewhere else."

"I wasn't moping."

"Okay. Let's recap, shall we? You walked in a little after midnight, trying and failing to close the screen door before the rusty hinges woke everyone up. Then you went to the bathroom and ran into a bed post on the way—"

"That bed wasn't there when I left."

"—then you knocked what sounded like a hair dryer off the bathroom counter. Then you plopped onto that creaky bed of yours. Oh, then you capped off your night by boo-hooing into your pillow while I sat there trying to keep Brie from snoring in my ear."

"That doesn't mean I owe you an explanation."

"You owe me something," Jess said. "An out-of-context detail. A play-by-play of the incident. I don't even care at this point. I just need something to make my lack of sleep worth it. What happened last night? Did the pair of you break up?"

"He and Loraine cornered me about something neither of them understands," I said. "I told them to f-off and now I'm here. The end."

"Your attention to details is amazing."

"I don't have to give you details. I don't have to give you anything."

Jess nodded, returning her attention to her bracelet. "So have y'all talked today at all, or have you done the avoiding thing? I didn't see him lurking outside the cabin this morning, so I'm guessing he's MIA."

"Of course he's MIA. He realized exactly what he was getting himself into and didn't need anything else to stay away. We're done. That's it."

"I don't claim to know anything about Grant, but I've talked with his guys enough to know he's a stubborn hard-ass," Jess said. "There're legends about him. How he almost burned down the mess hall when he was a camper here. How he almost got himself kicked out for good for skinny-dipping in the lake. He doesn't strike me as the type to just cop out because something got tough. There's more to this."

"That's it," I said, shaking my head.

"Explain it to me."

"No." I let out a long sigh and stared at the canvas. "I'd rather sit here working on this painting than talk about anything involving Grant. I came out here for a reason. You're messing it up."

"Fine. I'll be quiet," she said, putting her hands up. "Just one more thing first."

"What?"

She paused, meeting my gaze solemnly. "I've been with a lot of families, Alex. I've been passed around. I've been in and out of so many homes I've lost count, but I'm still here. I don't know what happened between the two of you, or why you think you're not good enough, but you are the most badass counselor out here. Don't let your screwups convince you otherwise. Or anyone else for that matter."

She tapped her fingers against the counter. "And I'll be here if and when you need to talk," she said, taking her bracelet with her. "Just bring some brownies with you."

She stepped away from the counter, shooting me a peace sign as she sauntered through the arts and crafts room. Out of all the people I thought could ever understand me, Jess wasn't even on the radar. Yet here she was, proving me wrong.

I returned to my canvas, trying to funnel my thoughts into the picture. Regardless of what happened between Grant and me, this conversation had left me with one thing: These kids weren't their labels. They deserved a second chance.

18

Let It Out

I left dinner that night, walking the path with my girls.

My conversation with Jess had me focused on getting to know these campers for who they were, not what their attitudes or stupid choices decided they would be.

"You're telling me Jess managed to do this whole thing by herself?" Brie said, glancing at her wrist.

Despite the occasional mix of colors and flaw in the pattern, I had to give credit where credit was due. Jess left our conversation and finished up the bracelet with zero help from me. It was better than anything I could make. Brie seemed to like it too.

"Why are you acting so shocked?" Jess said, nudging her in the side. "It's like you don't know how insanely awesome I am at pretty much everything."

"Okay, but you're the furthest thing from a crafter I've ever seen," Brie said. "Didn't you say you'd rather die a million deaths than do another thing of sand art? I could be trippin' but I'm pretty sure that was you."

"This isn't sand art," Jess said. "It's bracelet making, and I'm a boss at it."

We stepped onto cabin two's porch, still talking as the guys from Grant's side lingered outside their door. Curfew would be later on in the night, after another whole-group amphitheater hangout. If I was lucky, it wouldn't last long. I hadn't seen Grant all day, and being forced to be in the same place was the last thing on my want-to-do list.

"How long we got to get ready?" Brie said, pausing outside the door. "Enough time to curl my hair and do my makeup, or do I have to pick one?"

"We're supposed to be there right after dark, so you've got forty-five minutes. Whatever you squeeze into that time frame is up to you," I said.

"Makeup it is," she said.

I grinned and shook my head as she crossed the threshold, then scanned the outside of the cabin for any indication of Grant. He deserved better than me, but that didn't mean I didn't miss him. I could've used him today, when the world seemed to be against me, and I was once again on my own. But I could move on. I had to.

I crossed the porch and stepped into my side of cabin two, beelining for my bed, where my sketchbook lay on the plastic bin beside it.

"You sketching again?" Jess said, sitting on her bed.

"I started working on something about a week ago. I haven't had much time to finish it," I said, shrugging. "Since I had to leave that canvas in arts and crafts, it's the best I can do."

I flipped through the pages, bypassing the torn and tattered ones from my earlier counselor days. Those aggressively scribbled pages were a reminder of how bad things could get, when I kept my walls up and refused to let anyone in.

"Question," Brie said, pulling my attention from the sketchbook. "What are our plans for the Fourth of July? I know we've got a little under a week, but I like to pre-plan my outfits. I need to save the cutest one for that day."

"You act like it's a huge event," Jess said.

"Not as big as the camper talent show, but close." Brie looked at me again, brow arched. "Plans? You got 'em?"

"Nope," I said, shaking my head. "Loraine hasn't finished the schedule yet. I won't get it until the first."

"So you have zero intel."

"Um, I'm pretty sure I saw in the counselor cabin that we're doing something at the lake. Fireworks, maybe? I don't know." I grabbed a pencil from the bin beside my bed, mulling over where to go with the picture.

After trying for another thirty minutes to make something out of the mess of lines, I sighed and closed the book. Through the window on my right, the sun had disappeared beneath the trees. Dusk was here. Regardless of what I wanted, seeing Grant was imminent.

I slumped off the bed, letting out a long sigh as I faced my girls. My stomach was already spinning with anxiety, flip-flopping over things I couldn't change.

"We've got about five minutes before we probably need to head out," I said. "If you aren't done getting changed, doing your makeup, whatever, get it done or I'm leaving without you."

"I feel like that's directed at me," Brie said, staring at me from her spot on her bed.

That was a fair guess. Makeup palettes, foundation, and a handful of beauty products were strewn across her buffalo-plaid comforter, and she wasn't even halfway done with her eyebrows. If anyone was going to run us late, it was cabin two's makeup guru and her never-ending quest for the perfect brow.

I crossed the cabin, shooting her judgy eyes as I stepped outside. My breath caught in my throat, the sight of Grant leaned against the rail making me pause.

He glanced my way for a fraction of a second, a pained look crossing his face. I betrayed him by keeping my secrets my own. He knew it. So did I.

I brushed a hand through my hair and passed him, silent as I headed for the steps. He wore a pair of athletic shorts and a loose-fitting Texas Tech shirt. The brim of his hat shadowed his eyes, but I could feel him staring. Those hazel eyes drilled into me as I hit the ground, the notes of his body wash lingering across the porch, making it harder and harder to distance myself.

"Hey," he said, the line in his lips sharp and his voice so deep it was almost inaudible. "You planning on talking to me anytime in the next day, or should I chalk this up to a loss and move on?"

"You don't want me to talk to you," I said, still walking. "Just leave me alone."

"So then that's it?" he said. "You get to explain to me how you've done this terrible thing and I don't get to say anything in response?"

"Looks like it."

"Then you're a coward."

I turned, my blood heating at the insinuation. "You don't know what I am!" I said. "And you don't get to call me anything when you have no idea how hard it was for me to cut this thing off."

"Then why did you?" he said, crossing the porch. "Because you're afraid of what I think, or because you're afraid of what I have to say? You don't get to run away and hide just because you think you know what's best for everyone. That isn't fair."

"I'm not talking about this right now."

"Why? Are you afraid you'll make a scene?"

"No, I'm afraid *you* will," I said. I glared at him. The intensity in his voice set my nerves on edge. "I owe no one any explanation other than the one you got last night. I've said my part and I'm done. I'm out. Okay?"

"No, it isn't okay. It's a cop-out, Alex."

He landed on the dirt and his hand wrapped around my wrist. When I faced him, his look of disappointment burned through me. I did this. I did all of it.

"I'm asking you for one conversation to figure out how in the hell we went from caring about each other to you acting like my opinion doesn't matter," he said. "That's it. And I don't mean the kind of conversation where you tell me all these horrible things and decide I don't get a say in how I feel about them. I do get a say. I've earned that right."

"You've earned nothing."

"The hell I haven't." He let go of me, shaking his head as he paced the dirt. "From the moment you walked into this camp, I have done nothing but try to figure out a way to get past your wall of sarcasm and get to know the real you. I made an effort to figure out who you are, how you operate, and I ended up being the dumbass who accidentally caught feelings for someone who is too scared to let me in because they're afraid I'll judge them. That's not me, Alex, and you don't get to push me away because you think you know how I feel. *I* get a say in that."

"You don't get a say," I said, "because you don't know me, Grant. You know this girl, the one who acts like she has her shit together, but that's not who I am. I'm a mess. I'm literally doing everything I can to hold myself together, but I can't do that with you. You screw with my head."

"And you don't think you screw with mine?" He froze in his spot, his hands on his hips. "You're literally the biggest pain in the ass I've ever met. You waltzed in here with no experience and no clue what you were getting yourself into, and somehow I ended up being the one who got caught in the shuffle.

"That version of you that you claim is so screwed up has nothing to do with the girl I fell for. I care about *you*, Alex. I care about the girl I'm falling for. The one who puts me in check whenever I'm out of line. The one who makes me laugh when my temper is on the edge. You walk into a room and all I want to do is be around you, and you don't get to discredit that because you think the things you did have an impact on my feelings toward you. Your past is your past, just like mine is mine. That's it. That's where it ends."

"I killed someone, Grant. It doesn't just end." Tears streaked my face, hot against my skin. "You can stand there and tell me that none of this matters, but *that* does. That is a piece of me I have to live with, a piece I *chose*. You didn't choose that path. That path was chosen for you. You. Deserve. More."

"I want you," he said, his hand resting beneath my chin. He

rested his head against mine, the warmth of breath grazing my skin. "Did you force the keys into her hand and tell her to get behind the wheel?"

"What?"

"Did you?"

"No, but I—"

"Did you give her the alcohol?"

"I let her drive," I said, the words leaving me in a sob. "I got so caught up in what I had to lose that I lost sight of what we were doing. I was supposed to have her back. It's on me that she isn't here anymore. She could've been here if I—"

"She made the choice to get into that car," he said, his hand cradling the back of my head. "That's on her, Alex. It isn't on you."

"It isn't that simple."

"It is that simple. People make mistakes. Things happen and there are consequences. You're human. We're all *human*, and the longer you sit here and beat yourself up about what you could or couldn't control, the more damage you're causing. You have to let yourself heal. Get past this, because what you're doing right now is going to destroy you."

I swallowed thickly, my breath choked by sobs and emotions I never handled.

"I can't do this," I said, clutching my stomach as my lungs refused to work. "I let her die."

"Then we'll figure it out," he whispered against the crown of my head. "But we're doing it together."

19

Last Chance

"I can't believe that happened," I said as the swing in the pavilion rocked back and forth, creaking against the dark. My emotions were depleted, leaving me numb. Empty. But I'd survived the devastation of the truth. I'd made it out the other side.

I inhaled, my body shaking as my lungs filled with air. I hadn't cried like that since Nikki died. I hadn't let any of those emotions take a handle on my brain and just destroy me. I had tonight. In front of cabin two, with a group of campers looking on and Kira waiting in the wings to swoop in and take over.

She was with them now. Loraine would be here soon too, wondering where I was and what was going on. Waiting to give me some inspirational talk I really couldn't stomach.

"I think it was a good thing it did," Grant said, his arm warm against my shoulder. His fingertips raked the skin of my arm, leaving goose bumps behind. "There really isn't a right way *to* deal with it, but if you don't handle those emotions, they'll catch up with you."

"Like yours caught up with you?"

He nodded, his head resting against mine. He was silent for a minute as his long legs rocked the swing back and forth.

"It took me a good five or six months for it to sink in," he said. "Getting news like that isn't easy for anyone, but none of us were expecting to see a cop car roll up. I didn't expect to be sitting on a couch with my mom, listening to them explain how it happened. *Why* it happened.

"I knew what they were saying and everything, but that didn't make it real," he said. "I think I sat in that living room for weeks, waiting for him to stroll through the door. Waiting to see his smile. Waiting to hear his commentary on ESPN's NCAA basketball report. I just sat there waiting for him to come back, but he never did.

"It wasn't until the first basketball game of my eighth-grade year that I actually realized he *wasn't* coming back. My mom was by herself in the stands, looking lost in a crowd of families all there to support their kids, and he wasn't there. He wasn't relaxing in his stadium seat. Wasn't analyzing our opponent, or trying to give me a critique on my jump shot. And that was the moment I got angry. That was when it all went downhill."

"So what did you do?"

"Um, at first I did everything my mom wanted me to do," he said. "She thought I could go to a handful of family therapists and grief counselors, and they would help me sort out my feelings, but the more she pushed them at me the more pissed off I got. None of them realized how I felt. None of them had ever been there before. So, realizing I was pretty much on my own, I found a different way to deal. Drugs. Stealing. Anything I could do that would keep me distracted from everything I wanted to forget.

"Eventually, those distractions caught up with me. I got caught trying to buy some stuff from a dealer who was actually an undercover cop. He went after me and I ran. I was scaling a fence when he finally caught me. He pulled me off and I hit the concrete hard enough I broke my arm, but it didn't matter. I kept fighting him anyway."

"That's how you ended up here, isn't it?"

He nodded. "I was in a juvenile detention center for about six months before my mom discovered this place. Once she'd had a chance to check out the facilities and get a play-by-play from Loraine on how everything would go down, I got shipped out here for a last chance at getting myself on the straight and narrow. I think I went from pissed off, to even more pissed off, to *I'm going to get myself kicked out*, to thinking Loraine was the biggest asshat I'd ever met; but eventually I quit fighting everyone. I didn't have a choice but to get used to being here, so I got to know the people, started to realize I was making it worse for myself, and changed."

"Unlike the girl who was willing to go down swinging," I said, shaking my head.

"I dealt with it my way. You dealt with it yours. That doesn't mean anyone's way was better," he said.

I sighed quietly, letting the pressure off my chest. "It was easier for me to ignore everything and pretend I was normal," I said, blinking at the concrete in the dark. "Sometimes I think I even convinced myself I was. I would go see Dr. Heichman and listen to him try and talk to me about my feelings, but the whole time I was waiting to wake up and realize this was just a dream. Nikki was fine. She'd be at school on Monday, and we would finish out high school, planning out college and all the amazing things we would do."

I looked at him, guilt weighing me down. "I've never even gone to visit her," I said. "I must have driven by her memorial a million times, but I can't get myself out of the car. It's like standing there would make everything a reality. Like I can pretend it's just another cross on the side of the road, when it's more than that to both of us. It was the end of her life. It felt like the end of mine. Does that make me a terrible person, Grant? Am I a horrible friend?"

"You're neither of those things," he said, kissing my head. "You were doing the best you could to make it through. That's all you could do."

"I could've done more."

"You couldn't," Grant said.

He lifted his head, his dark brow furrowed and his hazel eyes filled with concern. "But I could've," he said. "I could've made you feel more comfortable. Done something to make you feel like you didn't have to keep your feelings a secret."

"I couldn't talk to anyone about it," I said, "and you couldn't have done anything other than what you did, which is be there. You're the reason I made it this far. Hard as that is to admit, you deserve some credit for putting up with me when I couldn't even put up with myself."

"I'll have to admit, it got pretty hairy sometimes. I wanted a counselor switch so many times I—"

I nudged him and he pulled me closer. The softness in his face contrasted the sharpness in his jaw and nose.

"Fine," he said. "I kind of liked being around you. Hard as it is to admit, I think you actually managed to knock me down a peg."

"You *kind of* liked being around me?" I said, facing him.

"I really liked being around you," he said. "And I plan on doing that as long as I can. As long as you'll let me."

I brushed my lips against his, the touch of his skin and the comfort in his kiss warming me again.

"We have the rest of the summer," I said.

"No. We have longer than that."

20

Promise

"All right, someone explain the rules of the lake to me," Brie said, standing on cabin two's porch, decked out in red, white, and blue and looking like Captain America's love child.

"I still don't have a good idea of what the rules are, and I'm not going to be the one to screw up and get myself sent home for breaking a rule I wasn't even aware of."

"No idea," I said, holding up my hands.

She shrugged and put her hands on her hips, shifting her sparkly eyelids toward Grant. "What about you? No answer from you either?" she said. "I thought you had the answers for *everything*. Your guys hyped you up like you were the camp GOAT."

"Bahh," I said, grinning.

Grant shot me a narrowed glare, but grinned just the same. "That's what a sheep sounds like, genius," he said. "And to answer Fourth of July Barbie over there, the rule is to stay with your cabin. If you go out of sight, it's a write-up and extra chores. Alex will be the one to pick and choose what they are."

"Oh, then I'm golden," Brie said, smiling.

She passed me, taking the steps two at a time. Jess and the other girls joined her at the bottom, the group on the porch rapidly depleting, much like the sunlight outside.

I turned, eyeing Grant up and down as he stood in the exact same spot where he stood every time we were here.

He wore a navy-blue polo and a pair of khaki shorts, his tan contrasting the hue of the fabric. Gone was his baseball hat. His messy brown hair was on full display, giving me a clear shot at his brilliant hazel eyes and sharp facial features.

I closed the distance once the stragglers were gone, raking a hand against the stubble on his chin. "Do we really have to go with them?" I said, looking at him. "It would be so much more fun to stay here and watch the fireworks from the porch."

"It's in the rule book," he said. "But no one said anything about sitting with them during the fireworks. Our job is to get them to the lake. We're in the clear after that."

He kissed me softly and I groaned, spotting Loraine as she walked by our cabin with a flashlight in hand.

"There goes the PDA police," he said.

"Meh. I don't know. I think she's so excited I finally opened up to someone about my feelings, she doesn't even care if there's PDA involved."

"You really believe that?"

"Not for a second," I said, grinning.

I grabbed his hand and tugged him toward the steps, mixing with campers from the other cabins as they walked the path toward the main entrance.

After camp was over and Loraine wasn't monitoring me, I could kiss him whenever I wanted. For now, it was probably better not to push my luck. Holding his hand was wholesome enough to appease her, but still got me the affection I needed to feel safe.

"So, how do all of these activities play out?" I said, holding his hand tighter. "I know we're supposed to go down to the lake and watch fireworks, but then what? Are we included in the post-party social, or is that limited to cabin one?"

"We get to participate," he said. "It's cabins one and two, and if we're lucky I'll be able to con Linc into covering for me so I can get out of there with zero camper responsibilities for the rest of the night."

"Do you ever do your job?"

"Nope. Most of the time I talk other people into doing it for me," he said. "It's a talent, really, and an amazing way to get myself an hour or two alone with you."

"Except I have patrols tonight."

"Exactly. We can get lost in the woods and no one will think twice about where we are or what we're doing."

I considered it. There was no one I'd rather do that patrol with. In the event of a snake, I could sacrifice him and run the other way screaming.

"I see you over there considering," he said.

"Yeah. Considering how I can sacrifice you to a snake."

We passed the counselor cabin, the light from the moon barely lighting a path through the thick canopy of trees. Fortunately, Grant knew where he was going. He bypassed tree after tree until we spotted the campers sitting among a series of flat-topped rocks facing the lake.

I caught him before we reached the tree clearing, my arms wrapping around his waist and dragging him out of sight.

"Hi there," he said, grinning at me. "I'm Grant. You are?"

"You know who I am and hush before you get us caught."

I peered around him, scanning the group for Loraine. Linc had her distracted farther down the shore. He might have been Grant's ally, but he was quickly turning into one of mine too.

"I heard from someone there's a geocache back here," I said, looking at Grant again. "It could be a rumor, but who knows? Maybe it's true."

"You lie, Alex Reynolds."

"I don't lie," I said, poking him in the stomach. "Check that app of yours and tell me you don't see a pair of coordinates for somewhere near this lake."

He grinned, his eyes on me as he dug in his back pocket and took out his phone. "If I can get service," he said.

The light from the screen lit the plains of his face, making them sharper, more defined. He was so devastatingly handsome it hurt to look at him, but he was mine. All mine.

"There's never been a geo—" he started, the corners of his eyes crinkling with excitement while the words died away.

"What was that?" I said, smiling.

"Alex, is this your way of telling me you found the Magic 8 Ball?"

"Linc did," I said. "Now it's *your* job to find it."

Grant laughed and shook his head, pivoting in the dark. It was a cheesy attempt at a date, but a girl had to take her opportunities when they came. If Linc was on board to help out, who was I to turn him down?

Grant wandered through the brush ahead of me, holding

back limbs as we walked farther and farther into the dark. The closer we got to the lake, the heavier the marine smell grew. The waves crashed against the rocks, lapping onto their eroded surfaces while moonlight reflected on the shore.

"What did he do, throw it into the lake?" Grant said.

"Is that something he would do?"

"Probably. He can be a jackass from time to time." He turned left after a moment, getting closer and closer to the shore. "Or maybe he isn't," Grant said after a minute. "Maybe he's just a better hider than I gave him credit for."

He squatted, peering beneath a dead tree curled up on the bank. He used the flashlight on his phone to light the area, then slowly pulled what looked like a soap box out from beneath it.

I closed the distance between us, watching over his shoulder as he popped open the lid. Inside, nestled atop a folded piece of paper, the key chain I'd taken from the Hobby Lobby geocache stared at him in the dark.

"Who would've thought you'd be a romantic?" he said, letting it dangle from his finger.

"Who would've thought a lot of things," I said, hugging him from behind.

He turned and wrapped me in his arms in a hug so tight I didn't want to let go. I could've stood beneath that moon, watching the waves lap against the rocks, forever, lost in a million possibilities and the one man who'd actually helped me see the way. But the summer would be over soon enough. We would go back to the real world, with no set of coordinates to lead the way.

"Where do we go after this?" I said after a minute, watching waves beat against the rocks. "When the summer is over and we're miles apart, is this something you'll still want?"

"I'm not going anywhere," he said. "I'll be in Lubbock, working on that sports-management degree, and you'll be in Louisiana, kicking ass and taking names, but we'll figure this out. I'll fly there and you'll fly here, and we'll be back in this place next summer staring at this exact same lake, feeling exactly the same way we do now."

A firework boomed above, crackling against the darkened night sky. I kept my eyes on Grant as an unbridled silence burned between us.

"You promise?"

"I promise," he said. "You're stuck with me, Alex. Personality flaws and all."

He brushed a kiss to my lips, the smell of vanilla and sandalwood invading my senses. Whatever this year would hold, whatever emotions lay ahead, at least I could face them knowing I wasn't alone.

I had this camp. I had Grant. In the end, that's all I'd really need.

Epilogue

"And that was basically my summer," I said, sitting forward in the oversized chair. "What do you think? Have I made progress?"

Dr. Heichman stared at me behind his glasses, his pen frozen against his notebook. He'd asked, "What did you do this summer, Alex?" and I'd given him the most accurate answer I could think of. If he wanted the shortened version, he should've given me a time limit.

He cleared his throat and set his pen down. "Well, it sounds like you did tremendous soul-searching," he said. "I'll agree there are still things for us to work on, but you're getting there. This has been a definite step in the right direction."

"It's been a leap," I said, flicking my attention toward the old-fashioned clock on the edge of his desk. I hadn't used up the full hour my parents paid for, but it was close enough. Much better than my pre-camp time.

He followed my attention to the clock, his brow arching. "Would I be pushing my luck if I asked you to continue discussing your summer?"

"That's pretty much it," I said, standing. "Went there. Came back. Currently trying to show everyone how much I've changed."

"That will take time."

"I've got plenty of it," I said.

I grabbed the complimentary bottle of water and walked across the room, pausing in front of the new portrait on the opposite wall. Gone was the horrible Rembrandt knockoff. In its place, a more colorful seascape.

"Who did this one?" I said, pointing to the painting.

"A local artist named Sczcotchy."

I glanced at the canvas again. The mixture of blues and greens captured the complexity of an ocean, while oranges and golds shimmered behind it, reflecting sunlight through the depths.

"I like it," I said. "It's good. Much better than the Rembrandt."

"I took your suggestion," he said, a small smile threatening his otherwise-neutral expression.

I grinned to myself and clutched the doorknob, opening the door to a mostly empty lobby. Inside, reading the newest *Good Housekeeping* magazine, was my mom, sitting in the same chair as always. She looked up from the pages, her eyes meeting mine.

"We're done," I said. "And I'm happy to report I made it almost the entire hour."

"Did you really?" she said, glancing at her watch. "Who are you and what did you do with my daughter?"

"Same me, just tweaked a little from all those Yoga for the Soul sessions I had to do while I was away."

"You did yoga?"

"Nope," I said. "I tried it once and was miserable. You should know me better than that."

She chuckled and tossed the magazine on the coffee table in front of her. Her heels click-clacked as we made our way to the exit.

Outside, late August's heat left everything sticky. My mom's car, parked along the sidewalk, glistened beneath the afternoon sun. The lights flashed to life as I reached the passenger side. She slid into her seat, buckling the seat belt as I reached for mine.

"Early dinner?" she said, pulling the car onto the same downtown street we'd driven a million times before.

"Long as it's Ellie's Café," I said. I shifted, taking my phone from my back pocket. A text from Grant had appeared on the screen. My heart fluttered. We were a couple of weeks from being out of camp, and my feelings hadn't changed. Maybe there was hope for us.

> **Grant:** Plane landed. I'll be on campus in less than
> fifteen. FaceTime date tonight?

"He make it safe?" my mom said, earning my attention.

"Currently on his way to campus," I said, typing out a response.

> **Me:** Only if we can coordinate with Ben & Jerry's
> **Grant:** And I'm taking a detour to United right now ;)

I stowed my phone out of sight. My mom's gaze was steady and unmoving. The idea of me having a boyfriend was still an adjustment for her, but Loraine had helped ease her and my dad into it. Who could make a better case than someone who'd known Grant since he was fourteen?

No one. Loraine was my best bet.

"So remind me: He's a freshman at Tech?"

"Sophomore," I said. "Sports-management major. I think he'd minor in business if he could, but rumor has it he's trying to get on as a manager for the basketball team this year. I don't think he'll have time."

"Sounds like he has a good head on his shoulders."

"Most of the time," I said, nodding.

I glanced out the window again, my heart cinching slightly. I wouldn't be able to schedule a visit until Thanksgiving break, but if we were lucky he'd come here in October. Until then, FaceTime dates and nightly phone calls would have to work.

Maybe it was better that way. I had to face my past here, and the people I'd neglected entirely too long. One person in particular.

"Would it be okay with you if I went out for a little while tonight?" I said, looking at my mom. "It will be max an hour. I just . . . I have something I need to do."

"What time you planning on leaving?" she said.

"Probably as soon as we're back. I'd rather get there before it gets too dark. I won't be gone long. Promise."

Her hands were tight on the steering wheel. She was still nervous when I went out after dark, but if she wanted me to change she had to give me the freedom to do it. I knew that. So did she.

"You can go," she said, nodding. "But be careful."

"I will."

* * *

Hours later, as the sun set behind a canopy of trees, I steered my car down the old country road leading to Baker's Swamp. The sky, streaked with vivid oranges and golds, contrasted the bitter memories of this place.

One held beauty. One held pain. Neither outweighed the other.

Silently, I pulled my car to a stop and took in a breath. My emotions balled at the base of my throat, the sinking feeling of loss heavy in my stomach. Too much time had passed, but I could do this. I had to do this. It was part of moving on.

Outside, a breeze ruffled the cypress leaves around me and brushed its way across my skin, sending goose bumps up my bare arms. Rocks crunched beneath my shoes, and then the path leading to Nikki's memorial shifted from pavement to newly trimmed grass.

It had been over a year since the accident, but the memories had yet to fade. Like the small white cross on the side of the road, and the fresh wreath of flowers someone had recently brought, this place and the person I'd lost here were more than a memory.

My arms crossed my chest as the stillness of dusk settled over me. There were so many things I wanted to say to her, so many things I wanted to apologize for, but the words wouldn't come out. I stood there, wrapped in silence as the events of the past year flitted through my mind.

There were still issues to work through, and emotions to handle, but at least now I had a starting point.

I had a second chance at living. I had the opportunity she never did, and I wouldn't waste it.

"I got this," I said, my voice barely a whisper on the breeze.

And I swear I heard her say, "I know you do."

Acknowledgments

To my editors, Kat and Holly, I thank you for being with me on this journey! Alex and Grant were just an idea, two characters I hadn't fully gotten to know, but both of you stuck by me as their story grew into something beyond what I thought possible. *Last Chance Summer* wouldn't be the story it is without you. Thank you for all your hard work! And to the rest of the amazing Swoon Reads team, thank you for all you've taught me about the publishing process. Working with you has been a wonderful experience. I hope I get the opportunity to work with you again!

To the readers, those amazing humans who took the time to pick up this book and get invested in Alex and Grant, thank you a million times over! I could never express how much your unending support means to me. I'm beyond grateful for you. You're the best!

To my husband, Allen, you've been there with me from the beginning. I could turn this into one massive and super sappy paragraph on how amazing you are, but I know you wouldn't want that. Just know how thankful I am for those all-nighters you pulled with me when I was up against a deadline. Know how much I appreciate you being there. Know how much I appreciate you being *you*. There is no one on else on this Earth I would rather do life with. I love you.

To Macy and Blake, go back to the beginning and re-read that dedication. Your dreams are always in reach, munchkins. Go out and get them. I'll be by your side no matter what.

To Mom, Travis, Greg, Wayne, the Hills, Ashley B., Stormy, and the rest of the crew, thank you! You're amazing. You're valued. I couldn't do this without you!

And last, but certainly not least, to Jenny, Jodi, and Fran— thank y'all for including me in your team! You ladies helped me multitask like no other and encouraged me when I didn't think I could fit anything else on my plate. *Last Chance Summer* wouldn't exist if it wasn't for your never-ending support. Thank you!

Check out more books chosen for publication by readers like you.

MATCH ME IF YOU CAN

Tiana Smith

All is Fair

DEE GARRETSON

The Birds, the Bees, and You and Me

Olivia Hinebaugh

A SOLDIER AND A LIAR

CAITLIN LOCHNER

BEWARE THE NIGHT

JESSIKA FLECK

MEET ME IN OUTER SPACE

Melinda Grace

SMALL TOWN HEARTS

lillie vale

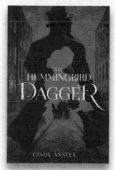

THE HUMMINGBIRD DAGGER

CINDY ANSTEY

YOU DON'T KNOW MY NAME

KRISTEN ORLANDO

LET'S TALK ABOUT LOVE

CLAIRE KANN

THE BRIGHT SIDERS

JEN WILDE

AUTHOR OF QUEENS OF GEEK

To Be Honest

MAGGIE ANN MARTIN